D1048977

Dear Mystery Lover,

Murder in Scorpio was one of last year's most praised first mysteries. Nominated for an Edgar Award, an Anthony Award, and an Agatha Award for Best First Mystery, Martha Lawrence is a major new talent.

Martha not only captures the sunny, offbeat appeal—combined with the danger—of Southern California, but introduces parapsychologist/private eye Elizabeth Chase, whose psychic abilities get equal time with her detecting skills. Nancy Pickard, author of the Jenny Cain mysteries, has this to say: "There's no tougher critic than a Virgo, and this Virgo says Murder in Scorpio is flawless." And Linda Barnes, author of the Carlotta Carlyle series, calls Murder in Scorpio, "a neatly plotted, fast-paced debut."

Martha will continue the Elizabeth Chase series using the signs of the Zodiac as her inspiration. Give Elizabeth Chase a try and I know you'll want to buy another copy for your favorite Scorpio.

Keep your eye out for DEAD LETTER—and build yourself a library of paperback mysteries to die for.

Yours in crime,

Shawn Coyne
Senior Editor
St. Martin's DEAD LETTER Paperback Mysteries

CRITICAL ACCLAIM FOR MARTHA
LAWRENCE AND <u>MURDER IN SCORPIO</u>

"An innovative and exciting new mystery featuring a private eye with a difference...Peopled with fascinating characters and a well-crafted plot, this is a terrific read."
—Janet Dawson, author of
Don't Turn Your Back on the Ocean

"Elizabeth picks up clues using a believable blend of investigative technique and psychic information. In the end, she convinces readers as skeptical as McGowan that, while some phenomena can't be explained rationally, they can be enjoyed by readers."
—*Publishers Weekly*

"Fine prose, a matter-of-fact approach to some rather extraordinary perceptions, and a wry sense of humor characterize a remarkable first novel."
—*Library Journal*

MURDER IN SCORPIO

MARTHA C. LAWRENCE

St. Martin's Paperbacks

MURDER IN SCORPIO

Copyright © 1995 by Martha C. Lawrence.

All rights reserved. No part of this book may be used or reproduced in any manner whatsoever without written permission except in the case of brief quotations embodied in critical articles or reviews. For information address St. Martin's Press, 175 Fifth Avenue, New York, N.Y. 10010.

Library of Congress Catalog Card Number: 95-34743

ISBN: 0-312-95984-2

Printed in the United States of America

St. Martin's Press hardcover edition/November 1995
St. Martin's Paperbacks edition/November 1996

10 9 8 7 6 5 4 3 2

To Mary

ACKNOWLEDGMENTS

A number of benevolent others have shared in the creation of this book. Many thanks:

to my agent, Gina Maccoby, and my editors, Hope Dellon and Kelley Ragland, for believing in Elizabeth and championing her adventures;

to a talented cadre of writers—Janice Steinberg, Abigail Padgett, Janet Kunert, Mary Lou Locke, Ann Elwood, Michael Peak, and Linda Page—whose whiz-kid insights improved the story;

to my buddies in law enforcement, George Brennan Hayes and Howard LaBore, who helped me keep my cop lore straight;

to my family and extended family—Clark Lawrence, Carroll Driggs, Chrissy Driggs, and the incomparable Thursday night group—for their unfaltering love and support;

and my profound gratitude to Deputy District Attorney Dan Goldstein, Detective Dianna Pitcher, and the Honorable Lisa Guy-Schall, for keeping me safe during the writing of these pages.

PROLOGUE

───

Fantastic as they may sound, the events in the following narrative are true.

My name is Elizabeth Chase. I saw my first ghost when I was an undergraduate studying premed at Stanford. With her smart blond bob and swaying hips, I assumed she was another student walking a few feet ahead of me along the cement path near Hoover Tower. Suddenly she turned and stared at me, her eyes as wide and black as a cat's in the dark. Then she simply faded, like the dying glow you sometimes see when you turn off an old television.

I was twenty then, old enough to worry seriously about my sanity. In an attempt to understand and resolve my sighting, I shifted all my attention to the field of psychology. I joined up with the Stanford Research Institute and spent the next ten years experimenting on paranormal subjects: precognition, near-death experiences, apparitions, telepathy. Along the way I earned two doctorates and discovered two things: 1) that paranormal phenomena are maddeningly hard to quantify, qualify, and explain; and 2) that my own psychic sight continued to sharpen, however much it refused to conform to laboratory schedules.

After research funds dried up in the mid-eighties I moved to Escondido, an inland suburb north of San Diego, and opened a psychotherapy practice. For a time I enjoyed assisting others in uncovering the mystery of their own psyches.

But soon I began to feel bored and uneasy, as if my therapist's chair had somehow become a raft and each day in it sent me floating farther and farther from my true purpose in life.

That all changed one morning over coffee and a newspaper. I spotted a picture of a freckled eight-year-old and the corresponding headline, "Search Continues for Missing Boy." Instantly an image appeared before me, a holograph superimposed above the paper: 929 IDLEWILD STREET. Ten years of research had taught me that such flashes, unprompted by the conscious mind, usually correspond in some inexplicable way to reality. I contacted the Escondido Police Department and reported my experience to the detective in charge of the case. He sounded less than enthusiastic, so I sat down at my computer to write a follow-up letter.

To my amazement two police officers appeared on my doorstep within the hour. With expressionless faces they informed me that a boy named Kevin Woods had been found, shot in the abdomen but alive, in an abandoned house at 929 Idlewild. They wanted an explanation.

Thus began yet another career. I now devote myself entirely to the use of my gift in solving crimes.

1

Sergeant Thomas McGowan was hardly the type of guy you'd expect to be consulting a psychic. Police officers generally can be divided into two groups: those who are willing to explore intuitive methods in the line of duty (an infinitesimal few), and those who think intuition is a crock (the vast majority). From his looks and reputation, anyone would figure McGowan for a member of the latter. Yet here he was, right on time for his two o'clock appointment. Standing at least six and a half feet tall, weighing at least double my one hundred twenty-five pounds, he virtually filled the doorway to my office. He radiated tremendous strength—and skepticism.

"Dr. Chase?" he asked.

"Please call me Elizabeth," I answered.

As if his gigantic stature weren't enough, he wore intimidating cop attire: a no-nonsense navy blue uniform, polished black oxfords, inscrutable mirrored shades. The gold badge pinned to his shirt gleamed white in the Southern California sun. Despite the sunglasses I could feel his eyes boring dubiously into me.

"Oh," he said, hesitating for a moment. "I was expecting someone older—"

"And shorter and fatter, wearing a multicolored muumuu and dangling earrings. Maybe even a turban?" I suggested.

"Yeah, something like that."

At least he admitted it. Psychics have it as bad as any minority in the prejudice department. You get pigeonholed into degrading physical and personality stereotypes, and people pretty much assume you intend to rip them off.

Considering it was Sunday, I thought I looked downright respectable. My khaki shorts were brand-new, and I'd even ironed a shirt for the occasion. It's true I was barefoot, but that's because the Hawaiian tradition of honoring the home by removing the shoes greatly appeals to me. I never wear shoes in the house, and I encourage visitors to leave their soles at the door as well. Staring up at McGowan's stony expression, though, I decided to let the shoe thing slide.

I motioned him through the door with a wave of my hand. "Step right in and make yourself comfortable. Would you like something to drink? Coffee or cappuccino?"

He took off his shades and lowered himself onto one of my overstuffed white sofas. "You tell me," he baited.

"Okay. Cappuccino."

I'd already prepared a couple of cups before his arrival. I now set them on the coffee table, smiled brightly at McGowan, and took a seat on the matching sofa to his right.

He stared at the steaming cups before us, then at me. His earnest brown eyes searched my face as if looking for suspects. "How'd you know?"

I took a sip from my own cup and shrugged. "I figured you'd want one. Inductive reasoning, basically. Most people will take cappuccino over coffee any day."

He nodded and frowned. So far he didn't seem to be having a very good time. From the look on his face you'd think I was about to sell him a time-share. "Can you read my mind?" he asked guardedly.

"Not at all," I assured him.

"Good."

He chuckled softly. I wasn't in on the joke, but he thought it was funny. He reached into the inside pocket of his jacket and handed me a picture that looked as if it had been torn from a senior yearbook. A gorgeous young woman with a mane of thick blonde hair and a wide, welcoming smile stared out at me from the black-and-white halftone photograph. I felt a palpable thunk in my stomach and knew at once she was dead. The light shining from the girl's eyes reflected something deeper than her obvious surface beauty. The word "tragic" crossed my mind, and a wave of sadness washed over me. I swallowed, then took a deep breath. Sergeant McGowan was watching my face with a blank expression.

"She's gone," I said as levelly as possible.

He narrowed his gaze. "Missing since last Friday."

"No, Sergeant. *Gone*. No longer in body."

At that the walls around McGowan came tumbling down. The intense brown eyes softened and the huge, muscular body relaxed. He now appeared to be what he really was—a human being inside a macho cop uniform. He blinked thoughtfully. "I tried to fool you," he said.

"It's okay, I'm used to it. Do you want to tell me what this is about?"

He stared, spellbound, into the cinnamony froth in his cup. "Lieutenant Gresham—that's my boss—thinks I'm going overboard on this case," he began. "Basically the consensus in the department is that it's your basic eleven-forty-four—fatality accident."

"And you don't think so."

"Well, no." He returned his cup to the table. "On the surface all appears kosher. Her name's Janice Freeman. She died last Friday in an accident out on Del Dios Drive—"

A road notorious for its eight-hundred-foot plunges, I thought silently.

"—and like I say, on the surface it appeared to be just another Del Dios dive." He looked at me sheepishly. "That's what the paramedics call 'em," he explained. "Anyway, an oncoming car crossed over the center line. She veered to avoid him and took the big plunge."

"Passengers?"

"None."

"What happened to the other guy?"

"His car rolled and he went down, too. Pronounced dead at the scene. Based on his blood alcohol, he never felt a thing."

Dappled sunlight danced across the coffee table. I turned to watch the breeze rushing through the sycamore just outside my office window. A heavy feeling had settled on my chest from the moment I'd held the girl's picture. I tried to send it away now, on the wind.

"It does appear rather open-and-shut," I said, turning back to McGowan. "Are you saying there's evidence to suggest she was murdered?"

"Evidence? No. Not yet." McGowan's eyes—objective, businesslike—met mine.

"But you have reason to believe it was murder."

A single frame of unmistakable pain crossed his otherwise impassive stare.

"Oh, I get it," I said softly.

"You get what?"

"You knew her."

He averted his gaze, found the window, and for a moment he too seemed to get carried away on the breeze. "We went to high school together," he began. His large irises flickered back and forth, as if he were watching a movie.

"I was a senior and she was a sophomore. By the end of the year we were pretty good friends. In my daydreams we were more than that, but—" He let the sentence drift off.

"But what?"

"Oh, you know. Her family was rich; mine was just working class. She spent her weekends at horse shows and yacht clubs. I spent mine delivering pizzas. So what, right? Doesn't mean you don't belong together. But by the time I figured that out I was off to college, so—"

I looked again at the sparkling eyes in the girl's picture. I wanted to tell him that Janice Freeman had possessed a beautiful spirit, but it sounded like the kind of thing you'd hear from a turban-wearer. So I translated. "She was a beautiful young woman," I said.

"Her looks weren't even the half of it," he answered. "She was a good person, a really good person, you know? You only meet a few of those people in your life. She was one of those." He pulled his eyes away from the window, over to me.

"Had the two of you stayed in touch?"

"No." A small syllable, full of regret.

I rephrased my earlier question. "But you have some reason to believe she was murdered."

He didn't respond. Instead, he studied the sunglasses in his hands, then began to fidget, opening and closing the stems.

"Something's got you spooked, hasn't it?" I asked.

He nodded.

"What?"

He released a long, heavy sigh. "Look, not to hurt your feelings, but I don't put a lot of stake in psychics. I feel kind of crazy even talking to you."

"I understand. That's a common reaction."

"You want to know what's got me really scared?"

"Sure."

"I'm afraid when I tell you why I'm here, you're going to think I'm crazy. Then what am I gonna do, when a bona fide nut thinks I'm nuts?"

2

I've learned not to take offense at the labels: kook, nut, weirdo, quack, flake, space cadet. Unfortunately there are enough unscrupulous wanna-be psychics out there to justify much of the public scorn.

"I wouldn't worry about your sanity, Sergeant," I said. "The mark of a true nut is that he feels perfectly sane and assumes the rest of the world is nuts. Your self-doubt strongly suggests mental health."

McGowan leaned forward and rested his chin on his hand, *Thinker*-like. His features were classically Irish: ski-sloping nose, strong jaw line, a thick shock of brown-black hair. With his enormous frame perched so politely on my sofa, he reminded me of the kind giant in a storybook I'd grown up with, although I had yet to see about the kind part. Now that he'd relaxed he looked world-weary but young, early thirties at most. He took a deep breath, then said, "Um, everything I say here is confidential, right?"

"Certainly. Unless it's evidence, which I can't withhold if I intend to keep my license. But you just assured me you had no evidence, so by all means, spill your story."

He hesitated before speaking. "You know, a year ago I'd have sooner knitted baby booties than go to a damn psychic. But something happened a couple months ago that—"

Once more he didn't finish his sentence. After a brief pause he started up again, this time determined.

"Okay, I've been on the force for over five years. I've seen a man shot in the face at point-blank range and live to talk about it. I've seen a man remain conscious—talking even—after getting shot clear through the head with a crossbow arrow. But what happened two months ago, I've never seen anything like it.

"I was off duty, driving home from a desert camping trip. It was about one-thirty in the morning—I like to drive at night, when the desert's cooled down. Anyway, I came across an overturned vehicle on Interstate 8. I was the first car to stop, so I radioed for backup. When I approached the car it was the damnedest thing—"

He shook his head, clearly still bewildered by the incident.

"The body had been thrown from the vehicle and the guy was obviously deceased—head severed at the neck. At first I thought it was another passenger standing over the body. But when I went closer I saw—"

He stopped in midsentence and seemed reluctant to continue. I waited. Suddenly McGowan looked directly into my eyes. "It was the *same guy*, Dr. Chase. He was standing there, looking down at his own body! I couldn't believe it. I kept walking toward him, kind of blinking my eyes. When I got about eight feet away he turned to me and shrugged his shoulders. Then he walked off—and disappeared!"

McGowan looked pugnacious now, ready to take me—or somebody—on. I smiled and nodded. "It happens."

"How?"

"I'm not sure."

"Why?"

"I'm not even sure of that. I just know that it does. And by the way again, you can call me Elizabeth."

"Right. Okay, so Elizabeth, you've heard of this kind of thing before?" His voice was practically pleading with me.

"Many times, Sergeant. Discarnate entity sightings are really quite common. It always amazes me how something so universal can remain so taboo. It's almost like sex in the Victorian era—as if putting enough shame and contempt around it will make it go away."

He nodded silently.

"So, how does this connect with the so-called Del Dios dive? Did Janice Freeman's ghost tip you off to her murder?" I asked these questions as straightforwardly as possible, but still they sounded sarcastic.

McGowan looked embarrassed. "Not exactly," he mumbled.

"Is there any connection at all?"

"Not a logical one, no."

A down-to-earth cop struggling with the inexplicable. I had to admit that part of me was loving this. McGowan did seem to be relaxing, though. He leaned back, stretched out his gargantuan legs, and asked for seconds on the cappuccino. Out of the corner of my eye I saw that his fully stretched legs extended a good foot and a half beyond the edge of the coffee table. I tried not to stare as I got up to refill his cup.

"Nope. 'Fraid there's no logical connection," he continued in a raised voice. "It's just that I've been picking up spooky things around car wrecks lately. I found out about Janice when a junior officer reporting to me turned in the paperwork on the accident. My high school heartthrob, dead. Hell of a shock. The kid had done a pretty sloppy job writing it up, so I went out to the scene of the accident myself." I handed him his refilled cup. He thanked me with a nod and said softly, "There's only one way I can put it. Standing there on the cliff where her car went over, I knew Janice Freeman's death was a murder."

The darkness surrounding her picture had been palpable, and I was fairly sure he was right. "Have you done any looking on your own yet?" I asked, as I settled back into the sofa.

"A computer check turned up that Janice had filed a

harassment complaint against a former boyfriend seven months ago. That's about it."

"Sounds like routine police work to me."

"Except that no one else in the department wants to play. What with the city's damn budget crisis, we've been understaffed the last three years. And the gang thing's making matters worse. Gresham let me know in no uncertain terms that I wasn't to be going after imaginary crimes when we had real ones to solve. I need help."

"Would my investigation be authorized by the Escondido Police Department, then?" I asked.

"No, you'd be working for me. I can give you a retainer of fifteen hundred dollars today to start."

I'd had a look at the EPD salary schedules and could probably guess within fifty bucks how much McGowan made each month. "Gosh," I said, "that's quite a personal commitment for a girl you knew briefly in high school."

"Um, it's not my money." McGowan was mumbling again. "Not really."

"Oh? Whose is it?"

He looked me straight in the eye. "You're really not going to believe this."

"Try me."

"That wreck out in the desert, where I saw the man standing over his own body? On a whim I took down the license plate number of the deceased's car and played it on Lotto. Jackpot—five grand. I'm not kidding you. You think this is all made up, don't you?"

I'd been staring out the window again, watching the wind pick up as the sky darkened. It looked as if we might be getting a June thunderstorm, very rare in Southern California. "On the contrary, Sergeant McGowan," I answered. "I think this is well worth looking into."

3

The rain began in earnest shortly after Tom McGowan left my office and continued right on through the next morning. We'd arranged for me to pick up a copy of Janice Freeman's file at ten. The parking lot of the Escondido Police Department overflowed with blue-and-white police cruisers, so I was forced to park across the street. I arrived in the reception area more wet than dry, but from the puddle on the worn gray linoleum, so had everyone else.

Two dispatchers manned the relentless phones behind the counter. Both were talking into their mouthpieces, but one saw me enter and invited me to sit by jabbing a pointing finger toward a row of chairs. The seats were the hard plastic variety you expect only at fast-food restaurants and bus stations. I hoped I wouldn't be waiting long. I had just become engrossed in a pamphlet instructing parents how to handle kids on drugs when McGowan walked through the door.

I looked up, and when our eyes met I felt one of those involuntary quivers in the abdominal region. *Uh-oh.* He might have felt it, too, because for a moment he just stood there looking at me, his outsized yellow parka trailing rivulets of rain. Then he spoke.

"Sorry I'm late," he said as he removed the plastic parka. "The cliché is true—Californians can't drive in this weather. Janice's file is upstairs. Why don't you wait in the employee lounge over here? The chairs are a little better."

I followed him through a hallway and into a room furnished with tables, sofas, and vending machines. While McGowan went to retrieve the file, I looked over a bulletin board plastered with flyers announcing police charity events and job openings. Several men and women in uniform sat talking and laughing together. A few of them hardly looked old enough to be out of high school, let alone enforcing the law with firearms and clubs.

Suddenly all eyes were on the doorway, where McGowan appeared with a distinguished looking man in a well-cut charcoal gray suit. McGowan provided introductions. "Dr. Chase, this is Lieutenant Gresham. Lieutenant, Dr. Chase."

I shook the man's hand, wishing that McGowan would stop with that "Dr." shit already. "How do you do, Lieutenant?"

Lieutenant Gresham could have been anywhere from a world-wise forty-five to a well-preserved sixty, with his dark silver hair and flashing eyes. "Fine, thank you—"

"Elizabeth," I interjected.

"Elizabeth. I heard about your work on the Woods boy case. Unusual. The media made quite a hullabaloo out of that one."

The case that had launched me into the psychic investigator business had indeed attracted an annoying amount of media coverage. Reporters had hounded me for weeks, until I finally discovered the effectiveness of answering all questions with boring monosyllables.

I scrutinized Lieutenant Gresham's face. Whether he thought me a jerk or a genius, his expression gave away nothing. "That's what the media do best," I answered with a smile. "The case had a happy outcome, anyway. His mom still writes to me."

I thought affectionately of Kevin Woods's mom, Theresa. "You are an angel of light," she wrote to me shortly after her son was rescued, "and for as long as I live, I will thank God every day that you brought my baby back to me. I can never repay you, but each day I will ask the Lord to bless you and keep you." I had sat with Theresa in the hospital waiting room while surgeons removed the bullet from her son's upper intestines. When they told her that Kevin was going to be fine, that he was conscious and asking to see her, I watched her face dissolve from rigid fear and agony into utter relief and joy. She threw her arms around me, laughing and weeping deeply by turns. Rocking her gently, I realized for the first time that I might be able to do something practical with my gift after all.

"I understand McGowan has you investigating the Freeman incident." The lieutenant was already glancing at his paper-thin watch and stepping away. Before I could answer he shot a "nice to meet you" over his shoulder and disappeared.

"The boss is kind of a busy guy," McGowan said, smiling apologetically. He handed me a manila envelope. "There's not a whole lot here, but it's a start."

"So how are you?" I asked, but before he could answer the Motorola two-way on his belt burst into violent static. He listened intently, apparently hearing words in what sounded to me like pure electrical noise.

"That's for me. Gotta go. Call me later at this number and the dispatcher'll page me in the field."

It was only ten-thirty by the clock on my dash when I got back to my car—perfect for reviewing Janice Freeman's file over a late breakfast. I pulled into Escondido Boulevard's modest midmorning traffic and headed home. For me, home and office are one and the same—almost. I live in a restored two-story farmhouse that was built in a field on the outskirts of nowhere in 1888. One hundred–plus years later, the house now finds itself in the middle of a growing city, at the corner of Tenth Avenue and Juniper Street. With the help of two friends—Nina, an architectural buff, and Connie, my connection in City Hall—I've arranged it so that the entrance to the office half of my house is located at (and listed as) 1426 Tenth, while the front door can be found on 3132 Juniper. Theoretically this protects my home life from the dangers and hassles I encounter professionally as an investigator. I don't think it fools anyone for a moment, certainly not the IRS, but it gives me a certain psychological comfort. The fact is, I'm too tight to rent a real office. I bought my house at the peak of Southern California's real estate frenzy, and its value hasn't exactly performed to the promises of the glowing appraiser. Historical as it is, I like to think its real worth transcends such banalities as the fluctuating real estate market.

I walked through the heavy oak door of 3132 Juniper and made my way to the kitchen table as best I could, given that Whitman, my seal-point Himalayan, managed to wrap himself around my calves every step of the way. I took a seat and pulled out the contents of the manila envelope. There wasn't much.

Two eight-by-ten black-and-white photographs depicted details of Janice Freeman's accident you wouldn't see in any newspaper. I've never been squeamish about blood or anatomy—probably the one qualification I do have for being the medical doctor my father so wanted me to be. I scrutinized the photos of what remained of Janice. Her long, lifeless body rested where the windshield used to be, half in the car, half on the hood. What struck me most forcefully was that Janice—the one I'd seen in McGowan's photograph—was no longer there. This was merely her empty shell. I scanned through the hastily penned entries of the accident report:

Day, Date, Time of Occurrence: Friday, June 5, 1992, 2200 hrs
Location of Occurrence: Del Dios Drive @ mile
marker 5, Escondido, CA

Victim(s): 1) Freeman, Janice:
Sex: F
Hair: Bld

                         Eyes: Blu
                         Race: Cauc
                      2) TBD: HMA
Type of Injuries: Fatal
Hospital Disposition: DOA

   Near the bottom of the report I found what looked to be a useful piece of information:

Next of Kin: Mr. and Mrs. Paul Freeman
               2005 Via del Cerro
               Rancho Santa Fe, CA 92067

4

Via del Cerro winds its way through miles of eucalyptus trees on a ridge of prime real estate in Rancho Santa Fe, California, a community that *Forbes* uncovered one year as having the highest personal wealth per capita in the nation. Situated ideally between the Pacific on the west and the desert on the east, Rancho Santa Fe enjoys ocean breezes without the coastal overcast, desert sun without the inland heat. A couple of Very Famous Movie Stars make their homes on this rarefied acreage, but it's not common knowledge. To Ranchoites high profiles are gauche, strictly the realm of the hoi polloi.

Taking in the splendor as I drove along Via del Cerro, I realized that I was still coming to terms with the fact that I had grown up here. A series of citrus groves and a couple of thoroughbred ranches lay between the Freemans' address and my old childhood home, so we hadn't exactly been neighbors. Chances were good that I had already gone off to college when Janice was a schoolgirl at Rancho Santa Fe Elementary. Still, I felt an odd connection with her. When I left this residential Disneyland at eighteen and entered the real world, I'd been filled with equal parts of guilt and terror. I wondered if Janice had experienced something similar.

The rain had stopped, which made my search a little easier. I slowed as I approached what I thought to be the general vicinity of the Freeman estate. There were no curbs here, and few of the houses were visible from the road. The covenant of Rancho Santa Fe allows nothing so crass as mailboxes. Residents (or their hired help) pick up their mail at the post office in town. Most of these spreads have no identifying information at all. Luckily for me, the Freemans' driveway was marked by a boulder larger than my car, tastefully engraved with the numbers 2005.

I turned up the steep drive overhung with towering eucalyptus and parked on the asphalt pad at the top of the hill. The sprawling mission-style house was too large to take in entirely from this vantage point. What impressed me most were the scale and variety of the landscaping—some of the trees were so massive they must have been a hundred years old. Walking along the brick path to the front door I passed a man weeding a vast bed of pale blue agapanthus. He gave me a nod and I said "Hi." I rang the doorbell—even that had a charming, unusual timbre.

The woman who answered the door stood in comical contrast to her elegant surroundings. She was short and grossly overweight. A blatant stripe of dark brown roots ran along the part of her garish orange hairdo. Her face, slathered in makeup two shades too light, was so pudgy it appeared to be rising like bread dough. She squinted up at me intensely, as if she were having a hard time seeing through her caky mascara. She kept squinting without speaking, so I started first.

"Hi. My name is Elizabeth Chase. I'm here on behalf of the Escondido Police Department to see Mr. and Mrs. Freeman." The "on behalf of the Escondido Police Department" part was what my mother would call stretching the truth. I considered it perfectly honest, in a vague kind of way.

"Ah'm Mrs. Freeman. Who're you again?" Her accent screamed Texas, and her attitude said "you're full of shit."

"I'm a private investigator working with the Escondido Police Department. I'm sorry—I understand you lost a daughter a few days ago. I'm looking into the accident."

She placed her pudgy hands on the immense outcrop-pings of flesh at her sides, where hips might ordinarily be. "That accident is none a yer damn business," she said tersely while shutting the door. Somehow my foot got caught in the doorway and the door bounced back open. "Paul!" she yelled in the direction of the back of the house, "Paul, you come out here right now!"

She stared me down with beady brown eyes until a tall, silver-haired gentleman in polo green cotton shorts, a white shirt, and sockless leather Top-Siders appeared in the entry-way behind her. "What's going on here?" he asked.

"Says she's from the po-*lice* department," the pudgy woman spit out with as much scorn as her Southern accent could muster.

I hated what I was about to do. "Mr. Freeman, hello. I'm Elizabeth Chase. I'm the daughter of Dr. Albert Chase over on Via de Fortuna?" I waved my hand in the general direc-tion of Fortuna, a road well known to any Ranchoite.

"Oh, yes." A pleasant recognition crossed his face, and he nodded and extended a hand. "I believe I met your father at the golf tournament last spring. How do you do, Elizabeth?"

"Fine, thank you. I'm sorry to disturb you here, but the police have asked me to look into your daughter's accident." I shrugged and added in my best golly-gosh voice, "I just happen to be a private investigator."

Mrs. Freeman's beady eyes had narrowed into hateful slits. I turned and smiled warmly at her.

"Come on out back to the veranda, dear," Mr. Freeman said. "We're having iced tea."

We walked through a series of antique-filled rooms, then out through sliding glass doors to a poolside patio with a view that must have taken in half of the county. I sat in one of the wrought-iron patio chairs and took the drink Mr. Freeman offered. It was barely noon and the iced tea was the

Long Island variety, par for the course in this neck of the woods. The alcohol odor practically punched me in the nose as I brought the glass to my lips.

"Ooo, sorry—I don't drink," I said, passing the glass back to Mr. Freeman.

"That's all right, admirable in fact," he said good-naturedly as he settled into a chaise longue. "Do we have anything nonalcoholic to drink around here, Annie?"

"Ah doubt it," she snarled, waddling off in a huff toward the house.

Paul Freeman wore a serious expression as he watched her retreat. "Please don't take my wife's behavior personally," he said. "Janice's death has put a tremendous strain on both of us. She's having a very difficult time coping."

I nodded sympathetically. Life may deal no greater blow than the death of a child. Yet even under these grave circumstances, Annie Freeman's hostility was excessive.

"So. I thought the police had finished their investigation." Two deep lines appeared between Mr. Freeman's eyebrows, and his mouth was set bravely. Pain leaked from every pore of him.

"I'm so sorry about your daughter," I said, meaning it. "My heart goes out to you. I'm sorry to be here dragging this out."

He dismissed that with another wave of his hand, but his Adam's apple pumped up and down and he averted his eyes for a moment.

"Officially, the police department is satisfied that Janice's death was accidental. But a sergeant on the force—Tom McGowan, a friend of Janice's from high school—isn't so sure. McGowan personally hired me to investigate further."

My words registered slowly, but when they did, Paul Freeman seemed to snap out of his grief. He looked at me anxiously. "What do you mean?" he asked.

"Was there anything going on in Janice's life that could have put her in danger? Any shaky situations or characters?"

A door slammed and we both turned to watch Annie Freeman waddle back toward us, glass in hand. "There you are, sugar," she dripped sarcastically, handing me a glass of plain tap water, no ice. It would have annoyed her, no doubt, to know that plain water was exactly what I'd wanted, but I just said "thank you" and let it go.

"Elizabeth here says there may be a possibility that Janice's accident was no accident, Annie," Paul Freeman said to his wife. "She wonders if Janice was involved with anyone shady."

"Well she certainly was," Annie Freeman declared. "Ah would put nothing past that *Alan* person." She dropped herself onto a chaise longue, her immense weight forcing a long, loud rush of air from the plastic pad—a noise that sounded remarkably like an embarrassing bodily function. We all pretended not to notice.

"Alan—?" I ventured.

"Katz," Paul Freeman answered. "A boy she met working at Pacific Properties."

"He's hardly a boy," Annie Freeman snapped.

"Well, all right," Paul conceded, "a young Jewish man. Bright but mixed up. Janice dated him for a time and had a little trouble breaking it off. But he's hardly a murderer, Annie."

"They worked together, you said?" I asked.

"Only for a short while," said Paul. "I believe Pacific Properties fired him."

"A San Diego company?"

"Yes. Janice worked a full-time job there, in addition to going to law school at night." The pain returned to his face. "She was a very proud girl. Never accepted help from us. Worked herself to exhaustion. Shouldn't have been driving Del Dios at that hour, but she did it three times a week, going home from class. I always worried something like this would happen." He took a long draw from his iced tea.

I turned to see Annie squinting viciously at me. "Alan

Katz is a shyster and a loser." A grin appeared on her little mouth. "If you land him in jail ah'll forgive you for ruinin' my day." The thought clearly brightened her mood. Her grin lingered.

"Do you know where I might find Mr. Katz at this point?" I asked.

Annie sniggered and opened her mouth to say something, but Paul cut her off. "Janice mentioned where he lived at one time, but I honestly can't recall. His former employer may have a forwarding address."

I made a mental note. My next question was the toughie. I took a swallow from my water and cleared my throat. "Um, do you have any personal effects of Janice's that you'd be willing to loan me for the duration of the investigation? I'll return them, of course."

"Personal effects?" Paul asked.

"Photo albums, correspondence, any personal papers would be useful. It would be very helpful to borrow something that was important to her—a ring or piece of jewelry, maybe."

"Jewelry!" Annie exploded.

Here it comes, I thought.

"What the hell kinda investigation is this?" she ranted. "Ah don't believe we saw yer identification, anyhow. Paul, don't be such a dummy! Who is this girl?"

I reached into my purse and handed her the wallet that held my private investigator's license, driver's license, VISA, American Express, library card, and all the other accoutrements of respectability. Paul was shaking his head and mouthing "I'm sorry" while his wife pored over my credentials.

"I work a little differently from most investigators," I explained. "Sometimes I have the ability to pick up information about people from their pictures or by holding something that was familiar to them."

Annie dropped my wallet on the cement patio like a hot

potato and heaved her bulk out of the chaise longue as if stung by a bee. "She's a witch, Paul! Ah want this woman out a my house immediately!" Her eyes were wide in her doughy face, her arms flailing hysterically.

"Now calm down, Annie, just calm down." Paul was doing his best to quiet her, but I could see it was useless.

"That's okay, Mr. Freeman," I said, reaching down for my wallet. "I'll just get going. You've been very helpful. I'll see myself out. Thanks again."

I walked back out the way I'd come in. The man in the agapanthus looked up and said good-bye very softly. I spent several minutes searching my purse for my car keys only to find them in my jacket pocket. As I started the car, Paul Freeman came up on the passenger side, carrying a cardboard box. I leaned over and rolled down the window.

"I'm very sorry about what happened in there," he said.

"No problem."

He slipped the box through the window and onto the passenger's seat. "These might be of help to you. I think Janice would have wanted you to have them."

"I wouldn't want to do anything against her mother's wishes," I said.

His earnest blue eyes locked onto mine as he leaned through the window. "Annie's her stepmother. I'm Janice's dad, and I say you should have them."

"Okay."

"Let me know what you discover. But for your own sake, contact me at the office." He handed me a business card. The logo of the famous restaurant would have been familiar to anyone over the age of three. Well, what do you know, I thought: *Paul Freeman, President.*

5

I had been a strange child.

My parents regaled friends and family with stories of my unusual behavior so often over the years that I eventually became immune to them. Like the child who's heard his father recount, for the umpteenth time, his bottom-of-the-ninth, pennant-winning home run story, I found the legends from my youth boring and embarrassing. It wasn't until I began studying psychology in earnest and comparing my childhood with others' that I was forced to acknowledge I was in a different league after all.

Perhaps the most dramatic of these childhood legends is the saga of the Bad House. Again, the tale has been told and retold so many times that it is difficult for me, even today, to separate genuine memory from images I may have fabricated from my parents' well-worn version of the story. After all, I was only three when it began.

Our young family had just settled into our new house in Rancho Santa Fe. My mother was making her rounds, getting to know the neighbors in a friendly, fifties kind of way. She proudly perched me on her hip and walked from house to house, ringing doorbells and saying hellos.

As Mom tells it, my screaming began—literally—the moment she set foot on the Dunwodys' driveway. At first she assumed it was ordinary crankiness, nothing more than a toddler's need for an afternoon nap. But I could not be calmed, and when Mrs. Dunwody opened the door my little fists pummeled the air and my screams bordered on hysteria. I repeated this obnoxious scenario on each of my mother's many subsequent attempts to visit the Dunwodys. Adults tried to reason with me, but I was intractable. Any mention of the house would produce a vehement string of "nooooo!"s and the admonition, "It's the Bad House."

I do not recall my screaming fits, but then I'm reluctant to remember a lot of my undesirable traits. To this day, however, my mind's eye can conjure a vivid image of the Dunwody house: imposing brick walls surrounded by air that feels too quiet, too thick. The house always seems to be cast in shadow, regardless of how sunny the day is.

My disturbing behavior put a damper on any friendship developing between the Dunwodys and my parents. This was something of a disappointment to them, as Ralph and Bobbie Jean had a daughter my age and they had hoped we'd be playmates.

Up to this point, the story is a little fuzzy in my mind and perhaps subject to distortion. But I lucidly recall the morning we all found out. I walked into the kitchen where my parents sat, speechless and shell-shocked, over the morning paper. Ralph Dunwody had made the front page by shooting his wife and daughter in their beds while they slept, then turning the gun on himself. I vividly recollect walking barefoot across the cool tile floor and announcing, "A scary thing happened at the Bad House." The next moment, too, remains as clear as if it had happened last week: the astonished looks on the faces of my parents as they stared at me, then at each other, then at me again. At the time it did not seem strange to me that I *knew*. I had just turned four.

6

The oleanders lining my parents' narrow driveway were overgrown and in full flower. A profusion of white blossoms engulfed my car on each side, so that driving through I had the sensation of being in an airplane, climbing through cloud cover. The property had been naked and new when we moved here thirty-some years ago. I now marveled that the bare little saplings I'd watched my father plant had gained such stature and beauty.

The front door, as always, was unlocked. I hollered hello and wandered through the back hallway into my mother's most likely hangout. Sure enough, there she sat, glued to her computer in the den.

"Mom?"

Facing the monitor, her back to the door, she was scrolling through data and answered me without taking her eyes from the screen. "I hear you, darling, and will be with you in one sec—" She highlighted a line of numbers and banged the Enter key with bravado. "There!" She spun around in her chair, arms outstretched for a hug. "Well, what a treat to see you, honey!"

I kissed the gray hair she'd piled haphazardly on top of her head. "Hi. Modeming again?"

"No, working on the newsletter. Hang on while I get out of this program."

My mother, Suzanne Sarah Chase, has for the last twenty

years amused herself in the financial arts. She currently publishes an investors' newsletter with a paid subscription base of five thousand or so. This passion for investing is an outgrowth of managing my father's neurology practice, which was transformed from a two-partner affair in the sixties into a twenty-member medical group in the eighties, largely through Mom's ability to make capital multiply. Although she holds NASD and State of California securities licenses, she's adamant that this is merely an avocation, that she does it "just for fun." Bridge, she'll tell you with a straight face, is her real job.

"What brings you home, hon?"

"Believe it or not I was in the neighborhood on business. Is Dad home?"

"He's in Boston giving an address at the AMA convention, remember? Did you need to talk to him?"

"No, that's okay. Hey, do you know the Freemans?"

"The Freemans over on Via del Cerro?"

"Yeah. Paul and Annie. They had a daughter about eight years younger than me, Janice."

Mom knit her eyebrows and wrinkled her nose. "Annie? No, I believe Mrs. Freeman's name is Ruth. Oh, wait a minute! Ruth Freeman died of cancer a few years ago. I remember they started a memorial fund in her name. She was rumored to be a hell of a bridge player, although I never played with her."

The computer suddenly purred and clicked, then let out an impertinent beep. Mom turned to the screen, which was flashing an amber display. "Oh stop it, you silly thing," she mumbled, flipping a toggle switch on the outlet at her feet. The screen went dark and the whirring faded to silence.

"Have you ever heard any dirt about the Freemans?" I asked.

"Nasty things? No, but then I'm not exactly a gossip. All I know is that Paul Freeman is a respected member of the business community. Why do you ask?"

"Their daughter died in a car accident last week."

"Oh, no!"

"Yeah, I know. It's sad. But there's something weird about it. A sergeant with the Escondido Police Department went out to the accident site. He smelled a rat and hired me to investigate."

"The police department hired you?" Her tone was incredulous. The use of psychics in criminal investigation is far from a commonly accepted practice, a fact of which my mother is keenly aware. For a time the LAPD had a written policy expressly forbidding such nonsense.

"They sort of hired me," I answered.

"What kind of rat did they smell?"

"Long story—I'll tell you later. The purpose of my visit is to pick your brains. Have you ever heard the Freeman family implicated in anything . . . unusual? Anything at all?"

"No, but like I say, I'm not active on any grapevines."

"Well, when you talk to Dad, can you ask him what he knows about the Freemans? Paul Freeman mentioned he'd played golf with Dad last spring."

"Okay. Hey, how about a little late lunch?"

"Sorry, Mom, but I'm itching to get my hands on a box of Janice Freeman's personal stuff that her father loaned me. I suppose there are instances where the trail gets warmer as time elapses after a murder, but I'll bet they're rare."

"No doubt you're right." She scrunched her shoulders in a mock shiver. "Ugh, murder! Your work is so grim, Elizabeth. Don't you find it depressing?"

"Depressing? Depressing is when people get *away* with murder." I grinned. "My work's a blast."

She responded to my statement with another cocked eyebrow.

"Good seeing you, Mom."

"You too, dear."

Halfway down the hall I heard her computer booting

back up and then her voice singing after me, "Pick some oranges on your way out!"

My house in Escondido is about twenty minutes from Rancho Santa Fe via Interstate 78, but I decided to take the long way home: Del Dios Drive. Winding through the southern-most foothills of the California coastal ranges, Del Dios had once been the only thoroughfare from San Diego County's inland communities to the coast. Janice Freeman's father had said that this was the route she took going home from law school at night. I wondered why, when the new freeway would have been so much faster.

Steep sage-covered hillsides climbed to the sky on my left. Like so many postcards, view upon view of the deep valley to my right opened before me as I wound through Del Dios's perpetual curves. I had once asked a Hispanic friend for his literal translation of Del Dios. "Of God," he'd replied. Del Dios Highway, Highway of God. The view, like God, inspired or intimidated, depending on one's perception of higher realms.

The well-banked road was nearly empty this pre–rush hour afternoon. I found myself stepping on the accelerator and having a very good time. Underestimating one sharp right hairpin curve, I pulled the steering wheel hard and the box in the passenger's seat nearly pitched into my lap. "Hello," I said out loud, slowing to a more reasonable speed.

I imagined for a moment what I would do should a car suddenly cozy head-on into my lane. I decided there wasn't a whole lot of margin for error.

7

Sitting cross-legged on my living room floor, I stared at the box Paul Freeman had given me. It was the brown cardboard variety, labeled with a black felt-tip pen in a feminine hand: *Correspondence 1991–92; Journals 1991–92; Civil Procedure I; Property II*. I was about to inventory its contents, but Whitman beat me to it. He jumped into the box out of nowhere and curled his lithe little body snugly onto the papers inside. His masked face gazed gratefully at me. I didn't have the heart to evict him just yet, so I contemplated the handwriting on the side of the box.

Technically, I'm not a handwriting analyst. I know nothing about the meaning of closed *o*'s and undotted *i*'s. But give me a handwritten note and I can read plenty about the author. The cursive script on the cardboard box was adorned with artistic flourishes, yet it flowed quickly in a no-nonsense manner. There were intelligence and generosity here. My guess was that Janice had labeled this box. Her stingy, suspicious stepmother had certainly not done the job.

"Okay, Whit, time to move."

He meowed in such a way that any idiot could hear him ask, "Why?"

I thought about his question and decided that I could indeed slide some of the stuff out from underneath him. I reached under his furry belly and pulled up a yellow spiral-bound notebook and a few thin booklets with blue covers.

The blue-covered booklets were apparently law school exams. I opened one labeled *Janice Freeman—Property II—Goldberg—3/22/92*. It was written in the same flowing hand, and I marveled that Janice could have maintained such delightful legibility under exam pressure. She was discussing *McMac v. Mary Lou*, demonstrating convincingly (to this layperson anyway) that Mary Lou was a bona fide third-party purchaser under something called a race-notice statute. Sure, the subject was boring, but I was amazed that the entire essay, written in ink, came to a conclusion without so much as one word crossed out. There were no grammatical errors, no misspellings.

It turned out that the substance of Janice's exam was as impressive as the style. "Extremely well done," the instructor—presumably Mr. or Ms. Goldberg—had written on the last page. "If this law school's rules permitted I would score this paper an A+." The other booklets contained similar praises from various teachers.

Scratch suicide over law school pressure as a motive, I thought.

The yellow spiral-bound notebook was thick, dog-eared, and doodled upon. I held it in my hands for several seconds. Unlike the exams, the notebook felt intensely personal. Holding it, I could almost sense Janice coming to life.

I have this theory about opening books. I'm not sure if it's genuine divination or just superstition, but it seems to me there are times when certain books open to the very page you need to read. This yellow notebook felt like that kind of document. I inserted my thumb at random and the notebook fell open.

JUNE 19

He's killing me. I love sex as well as the next guy, but these four A.M. marathons have got to stop. I thought men were supposed to pass out after coming! What drives him?

I contemplated that paragraph for several seconds, not without a few prurient visions, then turned down the corner of the page and flipped through the rest of the notebook. Janice had journaled religiously—not daily, but consistently. Her tone was so comfortable, so familiar with the process, that I suspected there were more of these notebooks somewhere, going back to her childhood, perhaps. Another paragraph caught my eye:

> JULY 17
> Stan offered me the operations director position today and for the first time in my life I turned down a promotion. I literally have 600 pages to read by next Monday—assuming I spend four hours/day studying & don't call in sick, I'll need to cover 25 pages/hour. Alan came by for dinner last night but left in a huff when I hit the books after sex. With all this going on, who needs more "management responsibilities" (i.e., baby-sitting) at the office?

I felt myself being drawn into the journal as surely as a television addict to a daytime soap. I set the yellow notebook aside. I would come back to it later and read it systematically from beginning to end.

I scratched Whit behind the ears and dug for more stuff, this time coming up with two file folders and a 1983 high school yearbook. I flipped through the pages, scanning the senior class photos, which were arranged alphabetically by last name. A corner had been torn out of the E–F page where Janice's picture would have been. I remembered the photograph Tom McGowan had shown me yesterday. Someone—Janice's father, perhaps—had torn out her high school picture and given it to the police. I didn't know what, if any, significance to attach to that fact.

The file folders were neatly labeled *Correspondence 1992* and *Miscellaneous*. For me this was like trying to decide between chocolate almond fudge and chocolate chip cookie dough ice cream. On the one hand, I love nothing more than reading other people's mail. Yet the mysteriously labeled *Miscellaneous* folder held equal appeal—who knew what lurked behind such generalities?

After a split second I dug into the correspondence file. A square, blank envelope lay on top. Inside was a card depicting an unflattering rear-end view of a real-life hippopotamus—not the world's loveliest of creatures, regardless of the angle. Inside, the card read: "Another Year/Big Deal." It was signed, "Happy, happy, Lou Ann." Paul Freeman had called his wife Annie. I wondered if Lou Ann could be her real name. It fit with the Texas drawl, and this card certainly smacked of her vile personality.

There were several postcards from various points on the globe, many written in a firm, square hand and signed, "Love, Dad." There was a thank-you note from someone named Joy, for "the hours I know you didn't have to spare that you spent helping me with Civil Procedure." There was a three-page letter from someone named Laura that began, "Dear Janice: I just wanted to take a minute or two to tell you how much your friendship means to me. . . ." The letter went on in that vein, peppered with phrases like "your courage and determination are an inspiration to me," "you are beautiful inside and out," and "I feel so fortunate to have you in my life." Underneath that was another envelope, this one postmarked July 21 and addressed to "Venus, c/o Pacific Properties, 1220 Waterfront Street, San Diego, CA." There was no return address. The card inside pictured Botticelli's version of the Roman goddess. Inside someone had written in plain, block printing:

You are:
   a. Too classic
   b. Too classy
   c. In class too often
Why don't you come mingle with us humans sometime?

The card was unsigned, but I had my theories of who'd sent it.

The last item in the file was a large, unmarked manila envelope. I pulled out an eight-by-ten color glossy and heard myself say, "Wow."

Janice was radiant. Head held back, long blonde hair falling loosely behind her, she clutched a man's white dress shirt around her torso and laughed into the camera. The shirttails grazed the tops of her long, tanned thighs and covered her hips but did nothing to obscure her lovely breasts. All this was enticing enough, but what really set her beauty apart was an absolutely unselfconscious smile. So often this type of picture offends or embarrasses, what with the model's contrived come-hither expression. This photograph exuded warmth, fun, and affection, as if this dazzling woman were your best friend. The Botticelli faded by comparison.

I suddenly remembered the police photograph of Janice sprawled across a shattered windshield. Silently, I sent her love and a vow that I'd do my best to bring her murder to light.

Whitman jumped down from the box and approached with a chirrup. He rubbed, mouth to cheek, against the sharp corner of the file in my lap marked *Miscellaneous*. "Let's see what's in here," I said. He sat patiently on the rug before me and waited.

"Ah," I said, opening the file, "looks like grown-up stuff." Inside was a black-and-white form embossed and stamped "FILED/Clerk of Superior Court." The words "domestic violence prevention" caught my eye. After studying this and several attached pages for a few moments, I deduced it to be a temporary restraining order, which the plaintiff, Janice Freeman, had arranged to be legally served on the defendant, Alan H. Katz, at 11:15 A.M. on November 11 at 1037 Silver Branch Road, Ramona, CA 92065.

This was beginning to look too easy, and it bugged me.

8

Before trotting out to Mr. Katz's last-known address, I thought it might be prudent to get a background check on the guy from the police department. Persons subject to a restraining order are legally prohibited from purchasing firearms, but for some odd reason they're always the ones who have Uzis tucked away in their closets. Just as he had predicted, Sergeant McGowan was on patrol when I called the station. The dispatcher told me she would page him immediately. I thanked her and hung up.

No sooner had I sat down again with Janice's journal than the phone rang.

"Dr. Chase?"

I recognized McGowan's voice. Again, a little involuntary thrill registered somewhere, which I did my best to disguise. "No, Sergeant McGowan, this is Elizabeth. When are you going to quit calling me Doctor?"

"When you quit calling me Sergeant, I guess."

Fair enough. "Well thanks, *Tom*, for getting back to me so quickly. And already I need a favor from you."

"Fire away."

"Could you run an Alan H. Katz through the computer for me? You should find a temporary restraining order."

"I already checked that out. Janice Freeman called us out to her place last December, claiming this guy Katz was violating a court order and harassing her. But the responding officer had to let Katz walk because there was no official restraining order in the system."

"What do you mean, no restraining order? I'm looking at a certified TRO right now."

"I'll check again, but I looked into that right after the accident. You say you have a certified copy of the restraining order? Does it have a case number and expiration date?"

"Yep. Case number 25923. Expires November 11, 1994."

"Proof of service?"

"Yes, sir."

"Hm. That's odd. Then again, not that odd. This isn't exactly state-of-the-art records management around here, just between you and me. A lot of things fall into a big crack between the courthouse and the law enforcement agencies, if you want to know the truth."

So many things the unsuspecting public doesn't know.

"How reassuring," I said. "Is there any rap sheet at all on this Katz guy? I've got an address for him here and I want to know what I'm getting into."

"*Elizabeth*"—he was either teasing or trying the name out slowly; I couldn't tell which—"I'd love to help you out, but I'm in the middle of some very important duties at the moment."

"Yeah? What's shaking?"

"Oh, you know. Eating doughnuts, pursuing petty violations of the law, that kind of thing. I'm afraid it'll be another forty-five minutes before I can get back to the station and run Katz through the computer for you. Sorry."

We were both chuckling as we rang off.

My kitchen clock read three o'clock. A netherland between lunch and dinner for most people, but then my eating and sleeping schedules have never coincided with the rest of humanity's. This was a problem for many years—being ravenous when everyone else was sated, just warming up socially when everyone else's eyelids were getting heavy. The freedom at last to capitulate to my own countersocial biorhythms is definitely the perquisite I cherish most in my new career.

A quick glance into the fridge polarized my choices: pizza of indeterminate age, or a drawerful of vegetables purchased yesterday. I love salads, but unless I'm in one of my rare Zen moods, I find the chopping part tedious and boring. I wasn't feeling particularly contemplative, but after lifting the lid of the soiled pizza box and taking a peek at the shriveled wedges within, I overcame my inherent laziness and opted for the salad.

In the midst of slicing carrots I dialed my attorney friend, David. He was my buddy long before he passed the bar, and he's one of the few lawyers I know who hasn't let the "Esquire" after his name turn him into an utter asshole. David is the guy who apprenticed me through my three-year transition from psychologist to investigator. Without his tutelage I would have never gotten my license. He knows this, of course, and uses it against me as often as possible.

The phone rang seven times before he answered.

"Hi, David. It's Elizabeth."

"Yeah, Liz, what do you want now?" I could hear him breathing heavily. I must have caught him on his exercycle again.

"Whatever do you mean, what do I want? To hear your sweet voice, is all."

At that he began to sing "The Star-Spangled Banner" at the top of his lungs.

"David, David! Stop! Refresh my memory. If a woman calls to report a restraining order violation, the cops have to pick the guy up, right?"

"See, you're so full of shit." He tried to sound hurt.

"I know I am. Just answer the question."

"Wellll," he drew the word out a mile long. "Technically, yes. In reality, not often these days. A restraining order violation is a misdemeanor. Unless the person being restrained is Atilla the Hun, the cops frankly can't be bothered. The jails are so full they're letting hard-core felons off with fines and work furloughs. Do you have any idea how many restraining orders are filed each week in this city? If they trucked every little TRO violator to jail—"

"I get the idea, David. Thanks."

"So that's it? You're done with me, just like that?"

"Let's just say I'll save some of you for later, okay?"

"Ooo, baby."

We could joke this way only because our relationship is firmly and comfortably platonic.

"I love you, David. Take care."

"I love you, too, sweetheart. Watch your ass."

I hung up and resumed slicing vegetables, trying to make sense of things. Janice had been troubled enough by Alan Katz to seek a restraining order. Obviously Katz had been a menace, otherwise a judge wouldn't have issued the order. But when she needed protection, Janice had not been able to get the restraining order enforced, which means that for all practical purposes it was a worthless piece of paper. Gee, what a great system, I thought. Kind of like Little Red Riding Hood trying to keep the wolf from the door with a stern note from her grandmother.

I was all the way through carrots, tomatoes, and green pepper when the phone rang again. The connection sounded as crackly and faint as an old gramophone.

"Speak up, whoever you are."

"It's your father, Elizabeth. Hang up and let's hope for a better connection when I call back."

Dad's image—deep-set brown eyes brimming with ingenious humor—flashed onto my inner movie screen. I smiled as I waited for the next ring. The second connection was mysteriously crystal clear.

"Fiber optics," he explained.

"So how's Boston, Dad?"

"As AMA conventions go, I'm forced to admit this year's

powwow is really quite stimulating. Neurotechnology is advancing at a rate that is simply mind-boggling, if you'll pardon the pun. We're going to have the scientific recipe for Thought itself soon, my dear."

My father and I share a fascination with the mind, but we come at it from opposite ends of the spectrum. He's spent his entire life exploring reality from the Matter Creates Thought angle; I've worked from the premise that Thought Creates Matter. I'm sure we both suspect that our positions represent the two sides of a single coin. Still, we enjoy antagonizing each other.

"Come on, Dad, thoughts are directed by *human will*. Have you come up with a formula for that yet?"

He just laughed. "Not yet, but stand by! Hey, Mom tells me you're investigating another murder."

"Yeah, well, we're not sure whether it was a murder or an accident. That's what I'm investigating."

"It's a shame, in either case. Paul Freeman is a very nice fellow, and I know that his daughter was the apple of his eye. Poor guy."

"He seemed nice. What else do you know about him? What do you know about the family?"

I know he heard me, but Dad didn't answer right away. When he did, he ignored my question.

"So you actually think the girl was murdered?"

"Think? No. Sense? Yes. There's something very weird going on here. But anyway, tell me about the Freemans."

Dad took a moment to clear his throat, then went on. "I know very little. I do know that the family is inconceivably wealthy. Disbursing their combined fortunes would be a career in itself. Whatever happened there, I doubt very much the motive was money."

"Combined fortunes?"

"The Freeman fortune and then the Hunter fortune. Paul remarried a billionaire in her own right, Lou Ann Hunter."

"But, Dad, she's a hick!"

"I'm surprised at you, Elizabeth. You of all people should know not to judge from appearances."

Busted. "You're right," I began. Just then I heard a beep on the line. "Oops, I've got a call waiting. Call me back if you think of anything else, okay? Bye, love you."

"I love you, too. Be careful, Elizabeth."

The call coming in turned out to be McGowan, who had found nothing, zip, zero on Alan Katz. According to police records, the guy was as clean as a whistle.

Records such as they may be, I thought grimly.

9

I was driving along Del Dios again, rhythmically climbing the winding road from left to right, left to right. It was dark now, the sage-covered hillsides shrouded in night. I looked to my right and saw nothing but sensed the vast depth of the valley below yawning into the blackness.

I don't remember how long I had been traveling this way, but I began to notice I was making no progress. Round and round Del Dios's curves I drove, but I was no closer to my destination than when I began. I stepped on the accelerator to no avail. The snaking road demanded concentration, but its endless curves, I knew, would never deliver me beyond this point.

Abruptly, I woke up. My eyes popped open, and I was fully aware of myself. I just didn't happen to be in my bed. The black of night made it difficult to see, but gradually I was able to make out the steep slope of a hillside a dizzying fifty feet or so below me.

I myself was hovering, weightless, in thin air.

This moment of recognition, I knew, held the potential for fear of falling. The fear would automatically activate some primal defense mechanism, and in an instant I'd return to my physical body.

But I'd traveled many times before and knew precisely what was happening. Following a technique I'd used successfully in the past, I willed myself to float to the right, to establish control. No problem. I sashayed sideways as easily as if I'd been turbocharged. It's an odd sensation. I always feel as if I'm one of those little high-priced, remote-controlled airplanes.

When I find myself out of body, there's usually rhyme and reason for both the place and the event. I've learned that if I ask questions in this state, the answers are often profound. Very deliberately and with a wide-open mind I thought, *What do I have to learn from this situation?*

The answer was not immediately forthcoming. I remained suspended and clueless. The moon hadn't risen, and the blackness was near total. Quite literally, I was in the dark on this one. With great effort I was at last able to make out the murky outline of a road cutting across the hillside below. The next question (*What do I have to learn from this road?*) had no sooner entered my mind than I became aware of activity directly beneath me on the hillside. Far below I could see two figures moving, so distant they looked like tiny toy soldiers.

I gave myself a mental command to move closer down, to see what game they might be playing. I descended with ease, gliding as effortlessly as any winged creature. The hillside drew nearer and I had a bird's-eye view of two men. They were talking, rather urgently, alongside a car.

I traveled closer and strained to hear what they were saying. For a fleeting moment I had the irrational fear that they might notice me, so I pulled up short. Then, without warning, everything went terribly wrong.

I lost control and had the sickening sense of losing altitude, fast. What followed was a frightening head-first plunge. I became painfully aware that my weightlessness was a thing of the past. Jostled and battered, I hurtled end over end in what seemed an eternal descent. I could hear the scraping of branches against metal, could feel the unyielding force of that unmerciful metal against my own bones. I tried to scream but had no access to my vocal chords. An immense and terrible pressure squeezed me in agonizingly slow motion.

I tried to move but couldn't.

Somewhere in the middle of my rising panic my eyes opened. I found myself rolled up tightly in the sheets and blankets of my own bed. Kaleidoscopic patterns of red and gray swirled in my vision, gradually giving way to the familiarity of my bedroom.

I sat up against the headboard, feeling queasy and sweaty.

The digital clock on my bedside table read 5:01. Far too early a rising time for my taste. I lay back on my pillow and tried to fall back into sleep, but a weight had descended on my chest like one of those radiation-proof smocks you wear getting X-rayed. The fearful mood of what I'd just witnessed hung all around me, and the phrase "impending doom" came to mind.

For several minutes I simply stared at the ceiling, reassuring myself that the sun would come up and the day would probably be as normal as any other. The pep talk didn't work. I continued to stare at the ceiling, where patterns in the plaster began to take on ominous shapes. Finally it dawned on me that I needed more light on the subject.

I wandered out to the living room and arranged three white candles and an incense burner around the African violets on my coffee table. The snap of the striking match reverberated in the early morning silence. The flame created a halo of brightness, which multiplied as each candle was lit. I then passed a stick of *nag champa* incense over each flame. A sweet calm enveloped me as the scent reached my nostrils.

The trees outside the window still looked black against the pale mauve sky of dawn. I sat on the sofa facing the eastern light and let my eyelids drop. Taking a deep breath, I focused inwardly on the spot in the middle of my forehead just above my eyebrows. There in the darkness behind my closed eyes a circle of light shone like some distant inner sun. I basked in its illumination, feeling the tension begin to slip from my body like running water.

I make it a point to go out of my mind at least once a day. Going out of my rational mind, I'm able to come to my senses—at least six of them. But meditating this morning wasn't easy. Frightful images from my nightmare buzzed in my brain like tenacious flies, bringing with them dreadful insecurities. I tried to push them out and force my mind to go blank. I grew weary from the effort.

Then a voice said, *Let them come.* And I smiled and remembered. Alan Watts once wrote that trying to push thoughts and feelings out of the mind during meditation is like trying to "smooth rough water with a flatiron." The trick is to accept whatever thoughts occur and simply listen to them as part of the general noise. Thus I gave in to the external/internal cacophony. It went something like this:

The hum of my refrigerator/the sense of hurtling downward.
The occasional songbird in my yard/the sound of scraping metal.
The soft sofa cushions beneath me/the bone-crushing pressure of the impact.

Soon my outside world and inside world came together. And a very aware, relaxed me woke up in the center of it all and thoroughly at peace.

When I emerged from my mediation, the anxiety surrounding my nightmare had evaporated. What remained were strong impressions—the dark hillside, the two men, the frighteningly real downward plunge. There was a message here, a warning, perhaps. All I needed to do was interpret it.

It was now nearly six o'clock, still too early to drop in on Alan Katz. I'd discovered quite a bit more about him, reading through Janice Freeman's journal last night. I'd paperclipped the pages that seemed to be significant. I decided to look those passages over again and figured I might as well do so from the comfort of my bed.

As far as I could figure, Janice had met Alan at Pacific Properties sometime back in February:

FEB. 14
Had lunch today with that hunk they hired recently in the prop. mngt. dept.—Alan Katz. He's freshly arrived from Hawaii of all places. When he told me where he was from I said, "Really?" and he goes, "What, just because I'm Jewish you assume I'm from the East Coast?" Had to laugh because he was right.

A whirlwind romance had quickly ensued:

MARCH 20
All Alan's cynicism melts away when we're in bed, and I melt right along with it. He's really nothing more than a curly redheaded overgrown cherub, and I told him so.

Clouds began to appear on the young lovers' horizon sometime that summer:

JULY 7
I'm so tired of feeling disappointed like this. Alan was a no-show again tonight. This is the second time in a week and I've had it. I don't have time for this shit! If it's another woman it doesn't make sense, because he's sending flowers and writing poems and making passionate love to me—when he's around.

AUGUST 22
I followed Alan home last Wed. because he broke another date and I was sure he was seeing someone else. He went straight home and started working in his garage. When it got dark I hid in the bushes . . .

(*A girl after my own heart*, I thought warmly.)

. . . but nothing happened, all night. No visitors. Just Alan
tinkering in his garage. I don't get it.

NOVEMBER 3

It finally dawned on me that Alan has a drug problem. Of
course when I ask he swears he never touches the stuff. Last
night after we made love and he fell asleep, I got his keys
and searched his car. I knew I was onto something when I
found a razor blade in a paper bag under the seat. It took a
while, but I finally found a stash of something that looked
like yellowish cocaine in a hollowed-out felt pen, also under
the seat.

I had to admire the girl's investigative flair. I also admired
the way she had handled her predicament. What was it her
friend Laura had written? "Your strength and determination
are an inspiration to me." Smitten as she obviously was, she
booted the guy and didn't renege. Not without a good deal
of anguish, though:

DECEMBER 31

I miss him. This pain reminds me of that compound leg frac-
ture (bone right through the skin!) I got falling off my horse
when I was 14. What did the doctor say? I'm afraid it's a bad
break, Janice, and it's going to take a long time to heal.

Alan, from Janice's accounts, did his best to keep the
wound fresh. It seems he refused to take no for an answer.

JANUARY 21

I can't even answer my own phone anymore. It's always him,
begging or accusing. He left seven messages on my voice-
mail at work today. The first three were I-love-you-I-want-
you-back, the last four told me what a bitch I was, why this

was all my fault, why *I'm* the one who has the problem. If he shows up on my doorstep again in the middle of the night I swear I'm going to press charges.

It was clear from this entry and others like it that Alan had become a royal pain in the ass, but nowhere could I find any references to violence or behaviors that would indicate a threat to Janice's life.

If Janice's accident had been a setup, who was the other victim, the guy who crossed over the center line? Tom McGowan had said the guy had been so drunk he'd probably never felt a thing. The coroner's report had confirmed that his blood alcohol had been .28, more than three times the legal limit. At the time the report had been written, the victim's name and address had not yet been confirmed. I made a mental note to follow up with McGowan on that.

The sun was well over the horizon now and I felt safe and warm. In a little while I could head out to the address where Alan Katz had been served his restraining order. I figured I'd let my eyes close for just a few more minutes.

10

The next thing I knew it was ten-thirty-five. If the adage about the early bird was true, I wasn't going to be getting any worms this morning. Fortunately this visit called for casual wear. I showered in record time, threw on a denim miniskirt and a Grateful Dead T-shirt, grabbed my zoris at the front door, and hoped my hair would dry by the time I got there.

Before starting the engine, I reached under the front seat of my car for my Thomas Brothers map to see exactly where "there" was. You don't go *through* Ramona to get to anywhere. It's one of those small California towns too far from the coast to be fashionable and too far from the interstate to be functional. The ubiquitous fast-food franchises have found their way to Ramona, but that's about it for modern civilization. The map confirmed that Alan Katz's place on Silver Branch Road was miles outside of a town in the middle of nowhere. I buckled my seat belt, reached for my box of CDs, and headed out of town.

Fifty-seven minutes, one Jupiter symphony, and a half album of Jimi Hendrix later I pulled into a dirt driveway marked by a beat-up, standard-issue gray mailbox. It wasn't quite noon, but the heat nearly knocked me over when I opened the car door. I got out and stood for a moment, casing the place.

The pink, flat-roofed stucco house sat like an oversized

shoe box on an empty desert shelf. Dusty beige backcountry stretched out in every direction. Whoever lived here wasn't big on landscaping. There wasn't a tree or shrub in sight, not a single patch of ice plant, even. The only green thing was a prickly pear cactus under the mailbox.

The front yard looked like the abandoned remains of a hundred garage sales. Every square foot was covered with junk—car parts, decaying furniture, rugs, toys, unidentifiable metal objects, crates, trash cans. Granted, there were no neighbors in sight, but if this was what the residents thought was okay to showcase out front, I'd hate to see what they had stashed in back.

A pregnant gray kitty was waddling cautiously through the junk. "Hey, Mom," I called to her as I walked past. She looked up at me and meowed, then took refuge from the heat in the shade of the narrow overhang along the side of the house.

I stood on the front step—an unadorned block of cement—and looked through the screen door. A gaggle of flies circled in the semidarkness of the living room, where the squalor theme so firmly established in the front yard continued in its indoor motif. I couldn't make out just what, exactly, was piled onto the floor and furniture. Suffice it to say there wasn't a clean surface in sight.

"Avon calling!" I sang out.

A skinny brunette hustled out of the murky interior and stepped up to the screen door. She, too, was dressed casually today: skin-tight denim cutoffs and a spandex top cropped just below her breasts. No shoes. I waited for an awkward moment while she smacked her gum and surveyed my T-shirt.

"What is this?" she demanded. Her voice was East Coast nasal, Jersey probably.

"I was just kidding about the Avon bit," I said.

She arched her brows with a look that roughly translated to "this better be good."

"Actually, Alan sent me out here," I ventured. Well, it was true, after a fashion.

Her face immediately relaxed. "Oh, come on in," she said, opening the door.

I stepped over the threshold.

"So, you wanna get stoned?" she asked.

I shrugged, doing my best to appear laid back. She turned and navigated through the mess into the living room area. I followed as well as I could.

Suddenly I knew where I was. This must be that mythical place, that legendary axis in the known universe where all lost objects accumulate. It had to be. On one small table alone I saw hairpins, a single sock, pens and pencils, a hand towel, keys without key rings, sunglasses, crumpled pieces of paper, a battery, a light bulb, a comb—

A hollow gurgling noise interrupted my reverie. I looked up to see the brunette sucking on a large blue glass bhang. She extended the pipe to me with a long, bony arm. "Wan' some?" she croaked through held breath.

"Hmm, naa," I said, as if I'd actually been debating the question.

My eyes had begun to adjust to the darkness and I looked around for a place to sit. That was when I noticed we weren't alone. A man, either asleep or passed out, was curled up on the sofa in the fetal position, his narrow butt hanging in our direction. I cleared some newspapers and clothes from a nearby chair and took a load off.

The brunette took another hit off the bhang. I was fascinated by her hair. Abundant and nearly black, it was gathered into a ponytail by one of those cloth accessories that look like wadded-up underwear. Her exotic eyebrows and wide, high cheekbones should have made her pretty, but a certain meanness outweighed her attractive features.

"What's up?" she asked.

"Not much," I answered. "What's up with you?"

She shrugged and took her gum out of her mouth. She

rolled the gum wad into a Zig Zag paper and tossed it on the table, then picked up a baking pan full of high-grade marijuana and began tearing one of the buds into small, pipe-sized pieces.

I tried to get a better look at the guy on the couch. Janice Freeman had referred to Alan as "a curly redheaded overgrown cherub." Whoever was dozing here had an unkempt mass of kinky brown hair hanging between his shoulder blades, and his vibes were definitely not cherubic.

I tried to think of a noncommittal opener that wouldn't reveal too much. I wondered who this girl thought I was—or if she even cared.

"So. What's Alan up to these days?" I asked.

"How the fuck would I know?" There was hurt in her voice.

"He's not around?"

She snorted. "Fuck no." She shook her head and rolled her eyes. "Fuuuuck no."

The atmosphere was thick with astral static and it was beginning to give me a headache. I took a moment to visualize a protective glass wall around me and silently called in for some spiritual backup.

"Yeah, well—" I stalled.

She reloaded the bhang without a word.

My head began to clear and I suddenly remembered a reference in Janice's journal, something about Alan having had a former lover, some girl whose name started with a *T* . . .

"By the way, my name's Liz," I said.

She looked at me dubiously. I hadn't exactly expected a curtsey and how do you do, but I'd hoped to at least pull a name out of her. No such luck.

"Yeah, right," she said. "Whatever." She flicked her cigarette lighter on, held the flame over the pipe bowl, and sucked.

By now the room reeked of pot smoke, with undertones of

filthy upholstery. The aroma of days-old dishes wafted in from the adjacent kitchen.

"So you and Alan have split?" I ventured.

She stared aggressively at me. Her bloodshot gaze was stoned but cold. "Listen, do you want anything, or what?"

I got that the "anything" meant drugs. "I need to talk to Alan," I said.

"Hey, I've got everything he's got." It was more of a whine than a statement, something you might hear out of a thirteen-year-old kid. I already knew she was too addicted and careless to make it as a big-time dealer, but from the sound of it, she took her budding entrepreneurship seriously.

"I'm sure you do. It's just that a friend of Alan's died recently and I need to return some stuff she had of his."

A little flicker of fear crossed her face. About time, I thought. Jesus, for all she knew I was DEA.

She put the bhang down and glared at me. "Hey, I don't know from Alan, okay? You got the wrong place, babe." She spit the words at me in an angry voice, and the guy on the couch stirred slightly. So much for mellowing out on pot.

I probably shouldn't have pushed my luck, but it had been a long, hot drive out here. "Well," I said pleasantly, "do you know where I can find him?"

She got to her feet and took a couple of steps toward me. For a moment she just stood there, glowering. Then she curled her lips off her teeth and repeated the words at shout volume. "Hey! I don't know from Alan, OKAY?"

She didn't add "get the fuck out," but she didn't have to. I heard it loud and clear.

11

I knew it had looked too easy.

It was now clear I was going to have to find Alan Katz the tedious way. I'm not the sort who can just close my eyes, put the tips of my fingers to my temples, and locate long-lost friends and relatives via some magic internal video scanner. True, I'd once saved an injured boy's life when the address of his whereabouts had flashed before my eyes, but the operative word there is "once." It hadn't happened before and it hasn't happened since. These elusive insights of mine are unpredictable and beyond my conscious control. They seem to be directed by a force, or forces, greater than myself. Either that or I simply haven't figured out the combination to my own subconscious locker. In any event, when I give one of my spectacular psychic performances, I don't count on ever being able to repeat it. It ain't show biz.

Some people will tell you that anyone can develop and hone his or her innate psychic abilities. People who make these claims are usually the same ones who will, for a small fortune, offer to assist you in this exciting process. There are ways to identify these people. First, they immediately recognize you as an "old soul." Next, they prophesy that your spirit is now ready for "a major transformation," and needs but their humble assistance to transcend its human limitations. Third, they make prolonged eye contact with you, their pupils full of hidden meanings. If you encounter such people, run. They are after your money or your body. I can guarantee they're seeking a tender exchange of one kind or another. And you will pay dearly for the "wisdom" they're proffering.

In my search for teachers who could explain my gift to me, I learned about these energy vampires the hard way. I once gave shelter to a gentle, wizened herbalist whose detailed reading of my past and present was so accurate it left me astonished, completely at a loss for words. I was even more flabbergasted the next morning, when I woke to find the herbalist long gone and my apartment picked clean. I wish that were the only example I could cite you.

I pondered the capriciousness of my on-again, off-again talent as I headed back to civilization along the remote, dusty stretch of Silver Branch Road. I was feeling disoriented and about as psychic as a brick. I'd managed to mask it, but the *Who's Afraid of Virginia Woolf* treatment I'd gotten from the lady of the drug house had put little fissures in my bravado. I was grateful I didn't get yelled at every day. Many people do, I suppose. A bit wistfully I remembered a screamer we used to have up at Stanford. Known among faculty and students as the Philosopher, he would roam the grounds in tattered clothes, screaming his ontological arguments to passersby, or simply yelling "Hei-degger!" at the top of his lungs. With his rangy body and impending forehead, the Philosopher had certainly looked forbidding, but his tirades somehow never left me feeling jangled. His screaming was impersonal, at the universe really, and in a way I think the entire university more or less empathized with his frustration.

But the lady of the drug house had indeed jangled me. I drove into the heart of Ramona—hard to miss, it's practically a single intersection—trying to shake that abused feeling. I detected a little self-abuse, too: I was silently chastising myself for sleeping late. I'd dashed out of the house without a great deal of planning—none, really—and now found the day nearly half over and myself without an agenda or an itinerary. I pulled up to a convenience store, hoping that a jolt of caffeine would at least begin to remedy my discombobulation.

I bought a large cup of coffee and immediately scalded the inside of my mouth. Should have known better. For some reason twenty-four-hour stores always heat their brew well beyond temperatures survivable by the human tongue, perhaps in an effort to make up for the lameness of the blend. I inhaled little baby cooling breaths as I headed for the phone booth in front of the store. The booth was that new cutaway style, and it provided no shelter from the gargling engines that pulled up. At least the inland county phone book chained to the metal shelf inside remained intact. I turned to the *P* section and estimated about a hundred and fifty entries beginning with Pacific. And this was the *inland* county directory. At the moment I was having a hard time recalling the name of the place where Janice Freeman had worked with Alan Katz—Pacific Something. No one will ever accuse me of having a steel-trap memory, especially for practical details. I gave up and dialed the Escondido Police Department.

To my delight the receptionist remarked that McGowan was "around here somewhere" and put me on hold. Mentally, I found myself back in one of the inhospitable plastic chairs in the EPD reception area, taking up where I had left off in the brochure about keeping kids off drugs ("Does your child have a new set of friends?"). Suddenly McGowan popped on the line.

"Elizabeth, you're amazing. You've solved the case already, haven't you?"

"Not even close."

"You're still amazing. Let's do lunch."

They were the kindest words I'd heard all day. "Let's do," I said.

McGowan suggested we meet at Akita, which surprised me. It's an unpretentious family-run Japanese restaurant between a dry cleaner and a dance studio in a strip mall on the south side of Escondido. I confess I pegged McGowan for more of a sit-down steak house kind of guy.

I got there first and waited on a bench outside the restaurant. I hadn't had time to stop home and change, and felt a little self-conscious about my denim mini and psychedelic T-shirt. His cruiser pulled into the parking lot and he waved when he spotted me. I apologized for my lack of professional attire first thing.

"Hi. Sorry I'm not really dressed—"

"I wish that were true," he deadpanned.

"You *what?*"

"I said, 'I wish I could get my foot out of my mouth.' " He opened the door for me, looking genuinely sorry and very cute.

"I thought that's what you said."

Inside we were greeted by a diminutive hostess, who bowed slightly and showered us with smiles and "herro-herros." McGowan towered over everybody, but next to our Japanese hostess he seemed to be from a different species altogether. Gracefully, he leaned down and spoke into her ear.

"*Konnichi wa,*" he said.

"*Ahh,*" our hostess replied, beaming up into McGowan's face and talking excitely, "*Konnichi wa! Ogenki desu ka?*"

"*Hai. Genki desu,*" McGowan replied.

She led us to a booth. When we were seated I said to McGowan, "*Konnichi wa?* For all I know you're saying 'the United States makes lousy cars.' But I have to tell you, I'm impressed."

He smiled and began checking off items on the menu. "It means 'good afternoon.' And I'm glad you're impressed. To be honest, impressing women at restaurants was my primary motivation for learning Japanese."

"No, you're better than that."

He caught the double entendre. "Honestly, I'm not. Both my Japanese vocabulary and I are very simple. My Japanese is limited to practical restaurant dialogue: 'I'm hungry today!' 'That tuna roll sure is good!' 'We need water here!'—stuff like that."

"I don't care. I'm still impressed," I said.

A young man brought two bowls of steaming miso soup. McGowan nodded to him, then said, *"Domo arigato gozaimasu."* I simply smiled at the young waiter, which seemed to get my point across just fine.

"You haven't solved the case, but you have revelations for me." McGowan picked up his bowl and sipped, his eyes meeting mine above the rim. Those eyes were heartbreakers—great warm brown things, full of soul.

"No revelations, really. A growing list of questions, though."

"Please feel free to probe." His eyebrows did a little cha-cha.

I pantomimed a disapproving scowl, then continued. "For starters, what was the name of that place where Janice used to work?"

I didn't blame him for the mock disgust on his face. "You're really on top of this investigation, aren't you?"

For a fleeting moment my astral travel trip—the view of the road from fifty feet up—flashed back into my mind. "On top of it? Absolutely."

"Pacific Properties."

"Of course." I quickly devised a little mnemonic cue, associating "properties" with a *proper* workplace where women had to wear panty hose. I hoped it wouldn't get filed in my brain under Pacific Panty Hose.

"Do you have any more information about the other victim in Janice's accident?" I asked. "The police report left a lot of blanks and to-be-determineds. Do you have anything more specific than 'HMA'?"

"Hispanic male adult."

"Ah, cryptic cop lingo. Okay, that's a start. How about a name?"

"Last I heard we were still trying to ID the guy and track down the registered owner. I'll have to get back to you on that. You think the other vehicle is important to the case?"

"I could be flying in the wrong direction, but for now, yeah, I think it's integral."

Our waiter brought a tray of colorful delicacies, a series of edible sculptures almost too aesthetically perfect to eat. We appreciated this culinary masterwork for at least two seconds before ravaging the plate.

I waited for a wasabi rush to clear my sinuses before asking my next question. "So you're sure there was no rap sheet on Katz? Any drug busts, in particular?"

"Not a thing. Why do you ask?"

"Drugs were the reason Janice dumped him. I found a bit in her journal, something about her finding a stash that looked like 'yellowish cocaine' among Katz's personal effects."

McGowan's face screwed into the picture of distaste. "Bad fish?" I asked.

He chewed vigorously and swallowed. "No, the sashimi's delicious. It's the mention of meth that turned my stomach."

"Meth?"

"The 'yellowish cocaine.' Crystal methamphetamine. Crystal, meth, speed, ice, go-fast. Poison by any name. It's San Diego's fastest-growing export and the most noxious drug out there by a long shot."

I'd heard of it, seen it mentioned in a few news stories. "What makes crystal methamphetamine so special? Isn't all that up-your-nose, into-your-veins stuff pretty noxious?"

McGowan popped a piece of maguro into his mouth and

closed his eyes in rapture. I studied his face. On a smaller man his features might have been too pretty. His eyes were enormous and beautiful, even when closed. He opened them suddenly and caught me staring. He smiled and picked up another deep pink strip of raw tuna with his chopsticks. It disappeared behind his lips and he devoured it slowly, with obvious pleasure.

"Elizabeth, why are we discussing something as repugnant as crystal meth over a delectable meal like this? The subtle flavor, the silken texture! There's only one thing better, you know." His eyebrows took a step, then waited.

"Because this is business?" I suggested.

The brows stepped down. "Very well, then, business. The business of crystal meth. Let me tell you a little story that I think will illustrate meth's special qualities. You know anything about the decomposition of the human body?"

"Only what I see in my mirror with each passing day."

"Visible only to you, I can assure you. Anyway, there's a whole field called forensic entomology, which is basically the study of which insects eat corpses and when."

"Mmm," I moaned with pleasure. McGowan frowned. "The sashimi," I explained.

"Anyway, there are basically five stages of decay and five waves of insects that attack a dead body. First you've got your necrophagous insects, good old flies and their larvae. Then you get your predators and parasites, like beetles. Then come the omnivorous species, ants being the primary example. And then there's what is referred to as the adventure species, such as stinkbugs and wasps—"

"We were talking about drugs," I reminded him.

"Patience, my darling, I'm getting to that. My point is that when bodies are found outdoors, coroners often hypothesize the time of death by determining which insect stages have developed."

"Got it."

"I have a friend who serves as a sheriff up in the hills and vales of Idlewild, one of the most kick-back posts to be found in police work anywhere. His entire career has produced only one good story, but it's a doozy.

"He got called out one day on an eleven-forty-six—a couple of stiffs found at a ranch house in the middle of nowhere. Seems these people had been brewing up a batch of crystal when one of the glass bottles in their lab burst. The way the hazardous materials team and the coroner reconstructed it, the guy standing in the room next to the bottle died instantly. His friend probably heard the explosion and poked his head in to see what was going on. He took in a lungful of the chemicals, ran about fifteen feet, and dropped dead."

"Is drug manufacturing usually this dangerous?" I asked.

"With crystal it is. It's made with hydriodic acid and ephedrine, a highly, and I do mean highly, explosive combination."

"Must be pretty lucrative for people to take that kind of risk."

"Lucrative? Street value's around twenty thousand dollars a pound. A decent lab will produce four hundred pounds a month. That's enough to induce a lot of scumbags to attempt better living through chemistry. Anyway, money is not the point of my story."

"But I'm going to hear your point soon."

"You are. My point is, the body sat outside—unprotected from elements, animals, and insects—for more than two weeks before it was found. During that time not one living thing—not a bird, not a fly, not a beetle, not an ant, not a stinkbug—so much as touched it. That's how toxic crystal methamphetamine is."

"Sounds like the bugs had more brains than the drug manufacturers did."

"A fair conclusion."

"Can we discuss something more pleasant now?" I asked.

"I'd love to."

"Who's paying?"

We ended our meal with plum ice cream and split the bill at my insistence. McGowan's car was parked closest, so we hovered there for a moment before getting on with our respective days.

"You still think Janice was murdered?" he asked. Solemnly.

I nodded. Solemnly also.

"You'll let me know when you've divined the murderer?" Half kidding now.

I leaned against the hood of his cruiser. "You'll be the first to know," I promised. Something between a heavy shudder and a slow pang traveled along my thigh, right where my flesh met the body of the car. For a minute I was puzzled. Up until now it had been McGowan, not his car, who made me quiver.

"I think you'd better take your car in for a checkup," I said.

The comment startled him. "I don't think so. It just had a tune-up."

"Maybe so. But this car is not happy."

"That's impossible," McGowan said, smiling brightly. "You're practically sitting on it. How could it not be happy?"

I turned quickly and headed for my own car. "Better check it out," I called over my shoulder. I never blush, but for some reason blood was rising in my face like gangbusters. I figured I'd better get out of there before McGowan had a chance to comment on my hot cheeks.

12

The office building of Pacific Properties had been designed to impress. The floors were marble, the paintings were original, and even the reception area commanded a view of the company's sparkling blue namesake. The young man covering the front desk inquired whom I wished to see in tones as smooth as velvet. I handed him my card and gave him a three-word reply: "Stan, about Janice."

After lunch I had stopped home to put my hair up, change into a respectable silk suit, and throw on a strand of pearls. I had even gone into my storage closet and exhumed an ancient pair of panty hose for the occasion. I tried not to wrinkle anything now as I waited on a supple leather sofa the color of French vanilla ice cream.

An eclectic magazine collection was fanned like a literary royal flush on the glass table before me. I was tempted to indulge my reading addiction but opted instead for the healing pastime of staring at the endless ocean. The sun was beginning its westward descent, and the oblique rays of late afternoon light shimmered hypnotically across the waves.

So this, I mused, was where Janice had met Alan, the roof under which their ill-fated romance had blossomed. I supposed the setting was romantic enough, as far as office environs go.

I tried to remember what else I'd read in Janice's journal about her job. Apart from the bit about her boss, Stan, offering her the operations director position, I couldn't remember anything specific. Most of Janice's journal entries had to do with life, love, and the study of law. She obviously didn't burn a whole lot of brain cells worrying about Pacific Properties after five o'clock.

"Elizabeth Chase?"

A man approached from the other side of the room. You could tell he wanted to be somebody by the slight swagger in his stride. He was impeccably dressed and his blond hair was combed in a manner that suggested frequent trips to the stylist. His eyes were large and oddly pale brown; his clean-shaven face bore the faint scars of adolescent acne. Yet his most notable feature by far was a violent red aura.

Thankfully, I don't often see auras. They're disturbing and distracting. Unlike Hollywood special effects, real auras are subtle and delicately translucent, like the barely perceptible halos you sometimes see around flames, or street lamps on a foggy night. Inevitably when I see one I rack my brains trying to figure out if it's an optical illusion, instead of just enjoying it for the rare sight it is. Even now I wondered if I'd looked too long into the reflected sunlight.

I tried not to stare as I got to my feet. "Yes, hello," I replied. We exchanged a no-nonsense handshake.

"I'm Stan Ellis. Come on back to my office."

I followed him through a hallway lined with more of the eye-catching artwork that had graced the reception area. I wanted to get a closer look at the paintings but couldn't tear my eyes off Stan's damned halo, which bobbed redly all around him down the hall.

We made a left into an expansive office whose floor to ceiling windows gave an unobstructed view of the ocean. The room was decorated in Italian ultramodern: minimal, refined, and, of course, black. I realize that this minimal black thing in decorating these days is associated with redefined elegance and neoteric sensibilities. But it all looks rather stealthy to me.

Stan took a seat behind his sleek, coal black desk. "We're still shell-shocked around here from the accident," he said shaking his head. "Are you a friend of Janice's?"

"No, I'm an investigator, like my card says."

With a peeved expression, he shuffled some papers on his desk and came up with the card. The muddy red corona around him blazed testily.

"Excuse me, Mr. Ellis. My eyes are very sensitive to the light. Is there any way you can close the blinds a bit in here?"

"No problem."

He reached to the corner of his desk and pressed a button. Slowly, with just the faintest sound of electrical assistance, the louvered blinds across the west wall of windows closed. The room dimmed, but the scarlet glow around Stan Ellis continued unabated.

"What kind of investigation do you do?" he asked guardedly. "You work for the government?"

"Basically, I'm a psychic. I do what any other investigator does, but I can sometimes bring a different kind of insight to a case."

He suppressed a smirk, trying to make his amusement look like puzzlement. Even under grave circumstances, people often find comic relief in the topic of psychic investigation.

"So you're not a friend of Janice's?" he asked again.

"No, I didn't know her personally. I've been hired to look into her death."

"Janice was probably the most competent employee this company has ever had. Anything I can do to assist you, just name it. I know we can't bring her back, but I hope someone is at least held financially accountable for that accident." His manner was civilized and his tone congenial, but the dark crimson aura suggested aggressiveness, anger, something primal.

"I'm looking into the possibility that Janice Freeman's accident wasn't an accident."

"Really." He raised his eyebrows. The paleness of his eyes gave him a vacant look incongruous with the intensity of his presence. The effect was disturbing.

"I'm afraid so. If I could just ask a few questions . . . this won't take long."

"Certainly. Go right ahead."

"Do you happen to know an Alan Katz?"

He looked up as if searching some top shelf for the answer. "Yes. He used to be an employee here. Why do you ask?"

"I need to ask him a few questions and don't seem to have the correct address. Would you happen to have it?"

"Sure, no problem." He reached for his phone and dialed a three-digit extension. "Carrie? Could you come in here a moment? Thanks."

The aura was beginning to fade now. I tried to let it go without resistance and stay focused on the conversation. "This sure is a nice office building," I said.

"Thank you. I laid the plans myself, with a little help from the architects, of course. It doesn't look fifteen years old, does it?"

"No, it doesn't."

There was a polite knock on the door. "Come on in," Stan called.

A young woman wearing an asymmetrical magenta haircut and a trendy frock took a few steps into the room. In spite of the hair, she looked sensible and intelligent.

"Elizabeth, this is Carrie Aimes, our personnel director. Carrie, this is Elizabeth Chase."

Carrie acknowledged me with a smile and a brief nod.

"Elizabeth is an investigator looking into Janice's accident. She needs Alan Katz's forwarding address, if you would."

"Ah," she began, "that's against corporate policy, Stan. Unless we have something like a subpoena we really don't give out that kind of information."

Stan frowned.

Carrie turned to me with an apologetic expression. "Sorry. If you give me your number I can call Alan and tell him you'd like him to call you. Would that be okay?"

"I guess it'll have to be okay," I said, digging in my purse for a card. "Thanks."

She took the card from my extended hand and turned to go.

"Wait!" I called out. "Can I just write something on the back of that, a message?"

"Sure." She handed the card back.

I pulled out a pen and wrote in tiny print on the reverse side: "If you are a curly redheaded overgrown cherub, please give me a call."

"Thanks," I said, handing it back. She glanced at my message and was shaking her magenta locks as she left the room.

"So," I said turning back to Stan, "what exactly does Pacific Properties do?"

He replied as if reading from an advertisement. "The company raises funds from institutions and individuals and invests those funds in high-quality commercial real estate. Our track record over the last seventeen years speaks for itself." He pulled some brochures from the shelf behind him and handed them across the desk to me. They were so slick they slipped through my hands and flopped to the floor like live fish.

"Oops," I mumbled.

He ignored my faux pas without missing a beat. "Pacific Properties currently has two billion dollars in assets under management, invested into more than nine hundred properties on the West Coast and in Hawaii."

"What kinds of properties did you say these were again?"

I'd interrupted his diatribe with a damn stupid question, that much was written all over Stan Ellis's face.

"High-quality commercial properties," he repeated in a clipped, deliberate voice. What a memory this guy had.

"I guess I was trying to get at what *kind* of commerce is conducted on these commercial properties," I said smilingly.

Stan Ellis sighed heavily, letting me know my query was wholly irrelevant. "Hotels, restaurants, convenience stores—" *What do you think, bimbo?*

"And when you say 'high-quality' properties, you mean . . ." As long as I was being dumb here.

"High-quality means our properties show a significant return on investment." This last Ellis stated in a tone you might use, for example, when explaining, *'No Trespassing' means keep your butt off my property.*

"Oh, I see." I glanced dutifully at the brochures before stuffing them into my bag. "And what did Janice Freeman do for the company?"

He smiled without revealing his teeth. I think he was trying to look kind. He looked strained instead.

"She did a lot of things. Added a lot of class, for one. Her primary job was to serve as a liaison to the investors. From time to time she was our emissary to the regulatory agencies as well—the Securities and Exchange Commission and all. Janice was quite a talented diplomat."

So basically Janice got to deal with customers and bureaucrats all day. Sounded like a thankless job to me.

"And how did she happen to get this job?" I asked.

"She applied," he answered with a smug grin.

I held my tongue and waited him out, looking expectantly into his face. In time he capitulated.

"Uh, if memory serves she came here fresh out of grad school with a business degree. Carrie may be able to give you specifics, her hire date, and so on."

"So, Mr. Ellis, you mentioned that Alan Katz was an employee here. Can you tell me anything else about him?"

"Well, not a whole lot, I'm afraid. I think he was one of the guys who did property maintenance, site checks, that kind of thing. He reported to my operations director, Marty White. Really all I know about the guy is that Marty asked me to authorize his firing. Yes, I remember now. He said Katz was a bright kid, he just didn't show up enough, is all."

Drug user, absenteeism—that part seemed to make sense.

"Were you aware that Janice was studying for a law degree?"

He smiled broadly, this time exposing a row of well-maintained teeth. "You bet. The girl was sharp. I'd make a decision and she'd find three or four reasons to go the other direction." He hesitated abruptly, as if recovering from a verbal blunder. "Not that she felt strongly about it one way or the other, mind you. That was just the way her mind worked, is all. She would have made one hell of a good lawyer." He pursed his lips tightly, repressing something. I wondered what.

"You would have hated to lose her to the legal profession, it sounds like."

"Pacific Properties is a big firm. We would have found a position for her on staff, I assure you."

Somehow I didn't think that's what Janice had in mind.

After a brief silence Stan spoke again. "Aren't you going to ask me if Janice had any enemies?" He sniggered nervously. "That's what they always do in the TV shows, you know, ask if they had any enemies."

I shrugged. "Well, did she?"

For the first time he sounded solid and sincere. "I can't imagine anyone not loving that girl. She could be a pain, but you had to love her."

"Did Alan Katz love her?"

He threw his hands up. "Nobody tells me anything. Is that the connection?"

"They were involved."

"Well I'll be damned."

"Anyway," I said, rising to go, "I'm going to go wait by my phone for Alan Katz to call. Thank you for your time and assistance."

As we shook hands the phone on his desk rang. He picked it up, barked hello, and listened intently. Immediately the red aura reappeared, bristling like the quills of a porcupine.

I turned to go.

"Carrie's office is the third door on the left, if you need more details," he called after me.

13

I had two choices for the drive home: the 78 freeway or Del Dios Drive. Charles Kuralt knew what he was talking about when he said that, thanks to the interstate freeway system, it was possible to travel from coast to coast without seeing a thing. I told myself I was taking 78 because I needed to get home as quickly as possible in the event that Alan Katz called. Later, driving mile after boring mile through depressingly homogenous freeway scenery, it dawned on me that the nightmare portion of my astral trip to Del Dios was still haunting me. I had taken the freeway, I realized, just on the odd chance the frightening plunge of the dream had been a premonition.

I exited 78 in Escondido and caught most of the lights green to Juniper Street. Until the freeway went in a few years ago, Escondido had still been just a farming community. The small-town atmosphere remains. On Tuesday nights the city cordons off four downtown blocks and holds a farmers' market where you can buy an armful of gladioli for two and a half bucks and locally mined tourmaline for a fraction of what you'd pay in any jewelry store. The population finally did reach six digits a couple of years ago, but Escondido as yet does not have the crowding, cost, and hipper-than-thou attitude of the cities along the California coast. I wasn't planning on moving anytime soon.

I pulled into the long driveway at the corner of Juniper

and Tenth. Getting out of the car I stopped to admire the bougainvillea climbing up the side of the house to the second-floor windows. The thick green leaves and deep pink blossoms stood out vividly against the white paint, a dazzling sight in the late afternoon sun. "Hi, you beautiful old thing," I said to the house.

I felt about this house the way I felt about my cat—not so much an owner as a caretaker and friend. William Faulker believed that the concept of owning land was preposterous. How could a man truly *own* anything that had existed long before he was born and would exist long after he died? I liked the idea that this house I now lived in had stood here before my grandfather was born. It reminded me not to take myself so damn seriously. After all, I was just passing through.

Whitman let me know with an upright tail that he was glad to see me home at a reasonable hour. I gave him several heartfelt pets before bounding upstairs to my bedroom to liberate myself from the dreaded panty hose and suit. My skin was so grateful for its freedom that I couldn't bear to punish it with more clothes. Heck with it, I rationalized, my underwear provides more coverage than most swimsuits you see on the beach these days.

There were no messages on my machine. Pest that I am, I put in yet another call to McGowan, who was out on doughnut patrol again. I left word for him to call me back, then spread out on the carpet for some asanas. The first few yoga stretches always feel strained and show me how separated I am from my body. By the time I'm through my routine, though, my body and mind are one: supple and relaxed, centered and calm.

I was in the plow position—head beneath my chest, legs stretched straight out, and feet touching the floor behind me—when the phone rang. I lifted my legs to the ceiling, rolled forward along my spine, and picked up the receiver on the third ring. My yoga teacher would not have approved of such a hasty unraveling. My jumpiness surprised me, and I made a note to slow down.

It was Tom McGowan, not Alan Katz.

"Where've you been?" I asked. "I thought you weren't on patrol today."

"I wasn't. I ran out for a quick errand and it turned into an hour-long ordeal. My battery died."

Well, well, well. "What a shock," I said.

"Now hold on. There's a perfectly reasonable explanation. You touched my car and the electrical system simply went into overload. Anyone can understand that."

"More likely the connecting cables were corroded and your mechanic overlooked them. I suppose you haven't had time to follow up on the other victim in Janice's accident."

"Not true. I've been working hard."

"Well?"

"The story, as told to me by the reporting officer, goes like this. He couldn't find any vehicle registration in the wreck's glove compartment. His next stop was the DMV. Based on the plates, the owner on record was a Mark Leffler of Pacific Beach. The RO went out to the Pacific Beach address and found Mr. Leffler very much alive and well. Leffler alleged he had sold the car about three years ago—apparently he'd forgotten to do a title transfer. Couldn't remember the buyer's name, either. So the RO posted a bulletin on the EPD's daily board and waited. Someone was bound to call in for either a stolen car or a missing person."

"How long did all this take?"

"About two days. Finally some scraggly character named Rob contacted the police. Said he was looking for his friend's stolen car. He claimed his 'friend' was the registered owner, Mark Leffler, but when questioned, Leffler swore he had no idea who this scraggly Rob guy was. So the officer put a little heat on old Rob, who finally admitted he hadn't purchased the car or obtained the pink slip and registration directly from Mr. Leffler."

"He bought a stolen car."

"That would be a reasonable supposition."

This was getting complicated. "So who was driving when the accident occurred?"

"Rob claimed that an 'acquaintance' had borrowed the car Friday night and never returned."

"He didn't know about the accident?"

"No. At that point we told Rob that his car had been involved in a fatal head-on collision. The guy had an absolute hissy fit that his car was totaled. Getting upset that his acquaintance was dead never seemed to cross his mind." McGowan ended the tale with a cynical chuckle.

"You find this funny?" I asked.

"I'm sorry," McGowan said. "It gets even funnier."

"Like what?"

"Like Rob insisted on being taken to the wreck. He wanted to pick it clean for usable parts."

"Lovely. Can you tell me where I can find this scraggly Rob character?"

"Yeah, when I get the paperwork. I'll try to get back to you today sometime."

"Thanks, Tom."

"So, Elizabeth, what have you got so far, if I may ask?"

"A lot of questions. I'll be able to tell you more once I get in touch with Janice Freeman's old boyfriend."

"Speaking of which, the courthouse finally verified that temporary restraining order against—what was his name?— Katz. It's in the police computer system now."

"Great. Perhaps the state should be advised that Janice Freeman is dead now. A certified restraining order is not going to do her a whole lot of good at this point."

I was expecting a witty retort, but McGowan answered me with silence. For a moment I'd forgotten that the corpse in question was his friend. "Sorry," I said.

"S'okay."

"Exquisite lunch," I said, changing the subject.

"Yes. And the food wasn't half bad, either. Let me know when you catch up with this Katz character. I must go. My beeper summons."

"Bye, Tom." Holy saccharine tablets, the guy was an incorrigible flirt. Question was, why was it working on me?

At the moment I had more pressing questions. First, if Alan no longer lived in the drug house in Ramona, was he in any way connected to the people now living in that dump? To that stone-cold hussy in particular? Second, did the red aura I saw around Janice's old boss have anything to do with her death? Third, who were the two men I'd witnessed from high above Del Dios Drive? And was my horrifying tumble a sympathetic flashback to Janice's accident, or just a particularly vivid nightmare? Or—I didn't like this thought—could it perhaps portend an impending crisis?

When Tom McGowan had first come to me with this case, I had felt strongly that Janice had been murdered. I was still certain of that but unsure of everything else.

I went to the cardboard box to retrieve Janice's journal. When I pulled out the familiar yellow notebook, a single loose sheet of paper fluttered to the floor. It was a photocopied page from some kind of legal review. I almost tossed it back into the box, but a headline, highlighted in neon green marker, caught my eye: "COMPANIES STEP UP EFFORTS TO QUELL FRAUDULENT REPORTING." The F word piqued my interest. I read on:

> With Securities and Exchange Commission enforcement actions for financial fraud on the rise, CFOs need to make a greater effort to prevent financial reporting abuses. Fraudulent reporting results from intentional acts or omissions that cause a material misstatement in the financial statements. The misstatements normally occur through deliberately overstating assets or <u>incorrectly accounting for revenues.</u> Corporate legal counsel

can help minimize the potential for lawsuits by reviewing the standards required by the SEC. . . .

Someone had underlined "incorrectly accounting for revenues" and penned an exclamation point in the margin. Pretty highfalutin language, I thought: "misstatements, overstating, incorrectly accounting for revenues." All sounded like cheating to me.

Most of the materials in the box had to do with Janice's law school homework—books, tests, notes. It was possible that this article was related to one of her classes. But Stan Ellis had described Janice as Pacific Properties's "emissary to the regulatory agencies." It seemed more likely that Janice had tucked this away for some work-related purpose.

I let my wheels spin on that one for a moment.

Next I placed the journal on the floor, stretched out on my side, propped up my head, and leafed through the pages. I was skimming for any references to Pacific Properties and for that passage I had read that had mentioned Alan's old girlfriend. Whitman made a halfhearted attempt to sit on the pages I was turning but soon burrowed alongside me, purring at full volume, his soft fur tickling my belly.

I eventually found another reference to Janice's job:

APRIL 22

Three more semesters and I'm out of Pacific Properties. I know it sounds naive but I really want to spend my life doing what I can to make the world a more just place.

I could relate to that.

"Three more semesters and I'm out of Pacific Properties." Stan, Janice's boss, had been so smug and certain that Pacific Properties "would have found a position for her on staff." My sense was that he wouldn't have stood a chance of keeping Janice, come hell, high water, or even exorbitant salary offers. Also, Janice seemed to be implying here that staying at Pacific Properties and making the world "a more *just* place" were mutually exclusive options. Which seemed to imply that Pacific Properties was not a just place. Which somehow didn't surprise me at all.

After considerable searching I found the passage I'd been looking for:

> APRIL 16
> It seems Alan has a past: a daughter from a previous union. She's six now and he goes on and on about how adorable she is. He doesn't get to see the girl often. He worries out loud about her some nights, says she doesn't live in the best of circumstances. I just listen—what do I know about kids? Only that there's no way I have time for them now or even five years from now. From what Alan says I guess his daughter's mother hangs out with a dealer in Ramona now and is more or less of a lowlife. Her name is Tanya.

I thought back to the drug house. Good heavens, could a child live in that squalor? I hadn't seen a little girl, but then it had been a weekday and she could have been in school. I remembered seeing toys strewn in the front yard. Of course, *everything* had been strewn in that yard. That bhang-sucking hussy, a mother? Sadly, it was all too plausible.

The ring of the phone startled both of us. Whitman leapt straight into the air and dove under the bed, all in an instant. At the same time I started, taking in a sharp breath. Why am I so jumpy? I wondered as I reached for the phone.

"Hello?"

"Elizabeth Chase, please."

"This is she."

"Hi. You were looking for a cherub? Red hair, curly, slightly overgrown?"

14

The voice on the other end of the line was smiling, suppressing laughter, even.

"This must be Alan Katz."

"And this must be a friend of Janice Freeman's."

"Yes, I suppose I am."

"Okay, I get it." I heard a low chuckle of amusement. "Carrie Aimes at Pacific Properties said you were a private investigator. And I almost bought it. Except Janice is the only one who's ever called me a cherub. Anyway, I'm intrigued. What can I do for you?"

Alan Katz had one of those deep, knowing voices that registered in the groin as much as the brain. A dangerous advantage for criminals and noncriminals alike.

"Would you be willing to meet me over coffee?" I asked.

"Oh, my. Very intriguing," he purred. "Ah, sure. When?"

"How about in a half hour?"

"Can't get free till eight tonight. Can we make it then?"

Damn. I had wanted to do this in broad daylight.

"Well, earlier would be better. Are you sure you can't manage it before then?"

"Yeah, I'm on a job right now. Sorry."

"Okay. Eight o'clock tonight will have to do, I guess."

"All right, where?"

"There's a Denny's just east of the Black Mountain Road

offramp on Highway 15." A very crowded Denny's. Lots of witnesses.

"How will I know you?"

That was a tough one. I'm of average height, average weight, and have dark brown hair of average length. "Let's see"—I paused here briefly—"how about I wear black boots and a black fedora?"

"Ooo. That's a little dressy for a Denny's, don't you think?" His tone was highly suggestive, as if I'd stated I'd be arriving stark naked.

"I'll mix it with jeans and a sweater. Believe me, I'll fit right in."

"Okay, Elizabeth Chase, see ya at eight." He hung up and the dial tone sang in my ear.

I didn't see anyone with curly red hair as I walked into Denny's. I paused briefly at the entrance near the cash register and scanned the tables, then took a seat at the counter and ordered a vanilla shake.

One vanilla shake and two cups of decaf later Alan Katz still hadn't showed. I was about to take a much-needed trip to the restroom when he slid onto the stool next to mine.

"Why didn't you just say you were gorgeous?" he asked.

Katz wasn't bad himself. Unfolded he must have been about six-two, lanky, but with naturally broad shoulders that stretched the confines of his plain white T-shirt. The way his pants fit he was a walking advertisement for Levi's jeans. His golden red hair was layered in loose, sexy waves that just grazed the edge of his collar. His pretty face was clean-shaven, but he didn't look like the clean-shaven type. I definitely saw mischief in his glittering blue eyes.

"That wouldn't have been specific enough," I answered matter-of-factly. "There are a zillion gorgeous women in Southern California."

"Believe me, you're a standout," he cooed. Such sincerity in those blue eyes. I could easily see someone buying this shit, even a smart girl like Janice.

"Janice Freeman—now there was a gorgeous woman." I threw out the bait and waited for tension on the other end of the pole.

The mischief disappeared as the corners of Alan's mouth turned down. "Janice is *the* most beautiful, period." He searched my face expectantly. "Do you have a message from her for me?"

"Can I get you some coffee here?" Our waiter appeared out of nowhere, startling both of us. The lower hemisphere of his head had been completely shaved, revealing naked scalp. The effect was somehow pornographic. A straight mass of ink black hair hung from the very top of his head, draping the left half of a face as white as chalk and about as enthusiastic. The circles under his eyes were as dark as bruises. How could life do this to someone barely out of his teens? I wondered. Alan and I simply stared at him, each waiting for the other to speak. I finally broke the silence.

"No more for me, thanks. Alan?"

"Ah, coffee—yeah, sure."

At the mere mention my bladder threatened to revolt.

"I'll be right back," I said, scooting off the stool. I slipped past some departing customers and looked back to see Alan watching me with a puzzled expression.

The restroom was barely larger than a good-sized closet and the air was thick with chemical deodorizer. I dove into the single stall and slid the lock shut. What did he mean, did I have a message from Janice? This was either an excellent cover-up or Alan was out to lunch. Perhaps both. I decided to follow wherever he was leading.

When I emerged from the back of the restaurant Alan was leaning against the counter, candidly watching for my return. He wasn't ogling my body, though. His eyes were searching my face, and I recognized the look in them: hope.

"So just what is it that you think I'm doing here with you?" I asked as I slid back onto my stool.

"I'm not really sure." He took a sip of coffee and grinned. He had probably seen his thirtieth birthday come and go, but when he smiled a pair of youthful dimples surfaced in his smooth, tanned skin. Together with a smattering of freckles across the bridge of his nose, the effect was boyish and highly disarming. "I can tell you what it is I hope you're doing here with me," he said.

"Okay. Go for it."

"I'm hoping Janice sent you to check up on me. See, I get it about the restraining order and all. Legally, I can't call her or see her. And under the circumstances it's probably not all that advisable for her to call or see me. So she sends a messenger, right?"

Our waiter plodded by and I signaled him, changing my mind about the refill.

"Am I right?"

"No. I don't have a message from Janice for you, not exactly."

He cast his eyes down but brought them right back up.

"Well, I have a message for her. Tell her I really have cleaned up. I know she won't believe that, but it's true. I've even been to some of those damn NA meetings." He rolled his eyes. "Actually they're not that bad. I just hate it when everybody holds hands at the end, you know? I get nervous and my palms sweat. It's embarrassing."

"I can't give Janice a message from you either, Alan."

"Well, you can tell her how I look, can't you? I mean, how do I look to you?" He leaned back, turned up his palms, and stared directly into my eyes, inviting a visual inspection. I thought he looked a little desperate.

"Okay," he went on. "Maybe I'm way off base. You tell me what you're doing here."

"Well, I *am* a private investigator." I retrieved a business card from my purse and wordlessly handed it to him.

He inspected it briefly. "Oh, man. She hired a detective." He laughed out loud. "I can't believe it."

"Actually, a sergeant from the Escondido Police Department hired me."

Alan snorted with disgust. "The police department. What is it now?"

Somewhere nearby some plates clattered to the floor and the unmistakable sound of shattering glass rose above the restaurant noise.

"Tell me, Alan, do you read the papers, watch TV, that kind of thing?"

"Not if I can help it. You watch too much of that stuff and you'll think the world is coming to an end."

"Alan"—I watched his face closely now—"Janice died in a car accident last Friday."

First he took a sharp breath, then he froze. His face started to blanch behind the tan. It felt to me as if someone had just opened a drain inside him and all his energy was slipping down and away. His head began to move slowly from side to side, then more assertively, as if he were refusing the knowledge like some unsolicited COD package.

"I'm sorry," I said.

He stared at me, horrified.

"If this is a joke—" he began, but he didn't end the sentence because something in my expression told him there was no point. A little whimpering noise escaped through his nose, and he suddenly bolted off the stool and rushed out of the restaurant at emergency speed.

I grabbed my purse, rummaging quickly. I threw a five on the counter and dashed after him.

As I walked through the door I saw headlights emerging from the L-shaped parking lot. The car approached very slowly, but when it passed I saw only a gray-haired couple in the front seat. I was at a disadvantage, not having seen the car Alan had arrived in. The spaces near the restaurant were well lit, and all the cars parked there appeared empty. I jogged down the parking lot, listening for engines and looking for passengers. As I rounded the corner I walked into near total darkness.

When my eyes adjusted to the night I thought I saw something on the driver's side of a Ranchero wagon about four spaces away. I approached cautiously.

A rounded form slumped over the steering wheel. It didn't appear to be moving. I walked slowly alongside the car and was just able to make out the loose waves of Alan's hair, now hanging limply around his bowed head. As I raised my hand to knock on the window, his broad shoulders shuddered.

"Alan? Alan, are you okay?"

The shuddering continued and I wasn't sure he'd heard me. I tapped the window gently.

He became still. Several seconds passed.

"Alan, just tell me you're all right."

I waited a full minute and then tried the door. It was open.

"Alan?" I said softly, leaning toward him. I put a hand on his back. He didn't look up. His head began to shake from side to side.

"Do you know anyone who might have wanted her killed?"

A low moan began to rise up from his hunkered form, gradually turning to deep, convulsive sobs. I put my other hand on his shoulder and waited several minutes for the worst of it to pass.

When he'd been quiet for a time, I spoke. "Are you able to talk now?"

He shook his head.

"Do you need a ride home?"

He shook his head again.

"Can I call you later?"

He nodded.

"Do you think you can give me your phone number?"

He sat up, as if this simple request had given him permission to put his grief aside for the moment. He opened the glove compartment, pulled out a business-sized envelope and pen, and wrote a number. He passed the envelope to me. I couldn't make out the postmark in the darkness, but I could see that it had been addressed to Alan H. Katz.

"You're sure you're all right?"

It was too dark to see his eyes, but the rigidity of his silhouetted features suggested that numbness had begun to set in.

"I'll be okay," he answered in a low monotone.

"Okay, Alan, I'll call you later. Take care, all right?"

I slowly retreated from him. As I walked past the rear of his Ranchero I paused to memorize the license plate number, just in case.

15

It had been a long day. Days beginning with nightmares tend to feel that way. A bubble bath was sounding really good about now, and I was tempted just to go home. But my client had requested that he be notified when I found Katz, and he deserved an update. I walked back into Denny's and called McGowan from the pay phone near the restrooms. Per the usual routine I gave the number to the dispatcher and waited for a call back.

A steady stream of bathroom-bound customers gave me dirty looks as they squeezed past me in the cramped hallway. With each opening of the restroom doors my nostrils were assaulted by a blast of air, the foulness of which was poorly masked by the cloying industrial deodorant. I had just turned my back on the whole unpleasant business and begun studying what was left of the ravaged Yellow Pages chained to the wall when the phone rang. I picked it up before the end of the first ring.

"Hello."

"Elizabeth? Did you talk to the boyfriend yet?"

"Yep."

"Did he do it?"

"Nope."

"You're sure."

"Yep."

There was a pause on the end of the line, as if McGowan was thinking about that. Finally he said, "I know nine o'clock is a little late, but I'm just getting off duty. Do you want to meet me at my place to discuss this?"

Following McGowan's directions and a couple of short-cuts I happened to know, I arrived about twenty minutes later. McGowan occupied a modest ranch-style house in the rural section of San Marcos, a community snuggled between Rancho Santa Fe on the west and Escondido on the east. My horse and I had conquered this terrain during my growing up years, so I knew the geography intimately. A dairy farm down the road set the tone of the neighborhood: Country, with a capital C. McGowan's driveway was easy to find. Bordering several dozen undeveloped acres, it was the only one along this stretch of road, certainly the only one with a police cruiser parked in it.

I got out of my car and stood for a moment listening to the night. The sounds out here were totally unlike those in town. The steady hum of traffic had given way to the rocking rhythms of field crickets. There were no sirens, no horns, just the wind shimmering like muffled applause through a curtain of eucalyptus leaves. This wasn't a tony address by society's register, but it was a fine place to live. I thought his choice in homesteads spoke well for McGowan.

I hit the doorbell and heard a series of deep, rolling barks inside, then McGowan's voice calling sternly, "Nero! Quiet!" The door opened and an enormous Rhodesian ridgeback burst through, his massive body wriggling dangerously with joy. Before McGowan could stop him the dog clamped his jaws loosely around my wrist in a slobbering canine variation of the handshake.

"The pleasure is all mine, Nero," I laughed. The hound lifted his face toward mine, his huge pink tongue noisily lapping the air. He wagged his entire body into me, nearly knocking me down.

"Nero! Heel!" McGowan grabbed the dog by his collar and jerked him back hard. "Sorry, he gets spastic when he sees a woman," he said.

I wiped the slobber onto the seat of my pants. "That's what I like about animals," I said. "They're so direct."

McGowan acknowledged my point with a twinkle from the corner of his eye, smiled ever so slightly, and said, "I'm going to put him out back. Enter if you dare."

I followed dog and man into the house, where a strong odor—something between nail polish remover and gasoline—hung in the air. A brief survey of the dining room table explained why. Spread across a blanket of newspapers were a shotgun, a rifle, and three semiautomatic handguns, all in varying stages of being cleaned. Moist rags blackened with gunpowder were heaped into a pile in the middle of the table. A bottle of Hoppe's No. 9 solvent sat nearby.

McGowan reappeared from the back of the house. He was stripped of his police regalia tonight. No uniform, no badge. Just a pair of old chinos and a short-sleeved knit shirt, yet he somehow appeared even more formidable than usual. Seeing him in the kind of clothes everybody wears, I got a sense how truly outsize his proportions were. Not to mention how truly proportional. "Very impressive," I mumbled unconsciously.

He, of course, thought I was referring to his other hardware. "Thanks," he said, beaming at the firearms on the table. "Do you know your guns?"

I laughed, feeling pleased that I'd finally gotten one by him. Still smiling, I shook my head. "I'm no expert. I've never had occasion to use one. So far I've managed to stay strictly on the investigative side of the business. I've left the actual apprehension of criminals to people like you."

He frowned, thoroughly unsatisfied with my answer. "So you don't know anything about guns—how to load, aim, fire, reload?"

"I passed the exam that the California Bureau of Security

and Investigative Services requires for a detective license, so I know the basics. And I'm licensed to carry a concealed weapon and all that Secret Squirrel stuff. But that's not how I work. I'm a sensitive, remember? Guns are just not part of my repertoire."

McGowan looked peeved. "Don't you feel a little vulnerable, not having a gun?"

"Put it this way. If I were on the police force without a gun, sure, I'd feel endangered. But I'm not a cop. I just . . . look into things. Besides, I have a guardian angel."

He started to roll his eyes but caught himself just in time. He took a breath and spoke patiently. "No offense, Elizabeth, but you sound naive. I'm sure angels are looking out for your soul, but sometimes you need a gun to cover your butt. These"—he indicated the tableful of artillery with a sweeping hand—"are my earthly guardians."

"Well, then, by all means please introduce us." What the hell, I thought. These things were obviously important to him.

McGowan grinned. "This," he said, reaching for the rifle, "is Mr. Winchester." He picked it up and placed it lovingly into my arms like some cherished mechanical offspring. A very high-tech-looking scope sat on top of its silk-smooth barrel. It was a big baby, weighing at least ten pounds.

"A little bulky for my taste." I peered into the scope. Through the lens the front doorknob thirty feet away came into focus as if it were inches from my nose.

"Let me show you the neato thing about this guy," McGowan said, relieving me of the rifle. "See this? This is a laser scope. Watch." He walked over to the back hallway and flipped off the light. "End of the hall," he said. I looked where he was pointing the rifle and saw a luminous red dot hovering on the far wall.

"Do you mean you just get that dot on your target and—"

"Practically impossible to miss with this thing."

"How about that black one there?" I pointed to the table.

The handgun was in pieces. McGowan quickly assembled it, pushing the slide onto the base. He shoved in the magazine and handed it over. "Here you go."

It was heavier than the thirty-eight I'd been trained to use but still surprisingly light for its girth. The smooth black barrel sat low in my outstretched hand. "This is a forty-five?" I asked.

"Yeah. Thirteen rounds, plus it holds one in the chamber."

"Very comfortable," I said.

He smiled with unmistakable pride. "It's a Glock—state-of-the-art technology. Sweet, isn't it?"

I removed the magazine and handed the pieces back to McGowan. "I'll bet that makes nice-sized holes during target practice."

"Oh, yeah." He lined up the sights on the television set in the living room and pulled the trigger with a loud, empty click. "Come on." He waved the barrel in the general direction of the sofas. "Let's talk."

The room was down-home comfortable, and the furniture, like McGowan, was enormous. I had to scoot back to support my spine against the sofa, my legs dangling straight out like a little kid's.

"I can't offer you a cappuccino, but I have plain old coffee on if you'd like some."

"Maybe in a bit. I'm still floating on the pot or two I drank at Denny's."

"How about a Klondike bar?"

"Ice cream I always have room for."

McGowan dashed into the kitchen and came out with a pair of square, silver-wrapped ice-cream bars. He tossed mine to me from about twenty paces. I reached up and grabbed it with one hand. When it comes to ice cream, I pay attention.

"So you met the boyfriend?" He unwrapped his ice cream and took a seat in a well-worn recliner.

"Yeah."

"And what makes you so sure he didn't have anything to do with Janice's death?"

I shrugged. "When you know, you know."

"What do you mean?"

"That's the nature of genuine intuition. When you receive an extrasensory truth, you just *know*."

"How old am I?" he asked out of the blue.

Out of the blue, a number and month appeared in my mind. "Twenty-nine," I answered without hesitation. "Last October."

McGowan regarded me with a poker face. "How much would you bet on that?"

"Your entire fee for this case."

A look of wonder crossed his eyes, giving him away.

"Are we on?" I asked.

He shook his head, resigning gracefully with a smile. "How do you *do* that?"

"It comes out of nowhere. This stuff totally circumvents logical thinking. I can't *will* it to happen. But when it does, it does."

"It must be kind of a nice talent to have," he said enviously.

"Yes and no."

"How do you mean no?"

"I can't say I enjoy the part about being branded a witch and a weirdo by some people. I know that deep down my detractors are acting out of fear, but it still hurts. I've had my share of hate mail. Most people, of course, hold me in only slight contempt, dismissing me as a borderline flake. Sometimes I get the feeling even you fall into that category."

McGowan couldn't disguise the fact that I'd pegged him. "You're right. Initially I had my doubts. But I must admit your little prognosis of my car today made me a believer. To tell you the truth, at this point I'm awed by you."

I could hear Nero scratching and whining at the back

door. "You're not without talent yourself," I reminded him. "Don't forget your experience at the accident site or your hunch to play Lotto with that license plate number."

"I've had experiences, true. But I don't pull birthdays out of thin air."

"Pulling birthdays out of thin air *is* an experience," I replied. "Besides, pulling a Lotto jackpot off a license plate isn't a far cry from pulling a birthday from thin air."

Nero whined piteously. "Aw, let him in," I pleaded. "He'll settle down."

McGowan got up with a sigh and headed for the back. Moments later the dog bounded into the room. He gave me a couple of sniffs with his wet nose and then turned to his master.

"So," McGowan said, resuming his seat in the obviously much-loved recliner, "suppose Alan Katz had been the driving force behind Janice Freeman's death. Would you 'just know' that, too?" Nero flopped down beside the recliner and McGowan absentmindedly patted his head.

"Like I say, I can't *will* these insights to happen. Sometimes I don't know. But I learned something about my sensitivity to psychopaths doing research work at Stanford a few years ago. I was interviewing a group of forty convicted felons for an experimental project in criminal psychology, recording their responses to a standard set of questions and jotting down my observations. These guys were in for a variety of offenses, everything from tax evasion to murder. But it was a blind study, meaning I didn't know what kind of criminal I was talking to.

"Anyway, during the course of one interview I began to feel uncomfortable, claustrophobic. This particular interviewee was handsome, well spoken, very cooperative. I tried to ignore the feeling and go on with my questioning, but the discomfort became so intense I started to have trouble breathing. Within a few minutes I was hyperventilating. My shortness of breath got worse and worse, and I ended up bolting out of the room in a panic. Turns out the guy I was interviewing was a serial killer, convicted of seventeen murders. He'd been indiscriminate about his victims—old, young, men, women—but he always used the same MO: suffocation."

McGowan said nothing, but nodded, taking it all in.

"So how'd you get to be a cop?" I asked.

A startled look crossed his face. "Me? Oh, I guess I always knew I'd eventually end up in law enforcement." He pushed his chair into a reclining position and laughed. "I had this natural talent for defusing fights when I was in school."

"It must be kind of a nice talent to have," I said.

He smiled. "Yes and no."

"How do you mean no?"

"Well, I can't say I enjoy the part about feeling like a bull in a china shop wherever I go. Being gigantic, you have to learn to be gentle. It's always the little guys who get into fights, you ever notice that?"

"I notice that the people who feel small inside tend to be the hostile ones, yes."

"I take it you still think Janice Freeman was murdered." We were changing subjects here, but not radically.

"I'm sure of that."

"So I guess the question is, who in Janice's life felt small inside, right?"

"We all feel puny by degrees. Janice had a boyfriend with low self-esteem, an insecure boss, an emotionally abusive stepmother, and a guilt-ridden father. In other words, she was an average, all-American girl."

"You've met all these people?"

"Yes."

"Did any of them make you feel sick?"

I laughed. "It's not always that obvious."

McGowan had stopped patting the dog's head. Nero sat up, a disappointed expression on his muzzle. He flopped his face onto his master's lap, hinting strongly for seconds on the head rub. As McGowan scratched behind Nero's ears and massaged his neck, the dog closed his eyes in rapture. I put myself in Nero's paws and vicariously enjoyed the thrill of McGowan's petting. For several moments there was complete silence in the room. Then the damn phone rang.

"Excuse me," McGowan said, heading for the kitchen.

Leave me alone in a room and I snoop—I can't help it. As soon as McGowan disappeared I cased the place. One wall was almost entirely covered by bookshelves. I walked over to survey the spines. What I saw amazed me. McGowan had amassed a respectable library of English and American literature, arranged alphabetically by author. My eyes scanned the top shelves: Audubon, Austin, Bellow, Burroughs, Carroll, Cummings, Dickinson, Eliot, Emerson. . . . I moved to the other end of the shelves, where the titles concluded, retaining their noble order: Vonnegut, Walker, Webster, Whitman, Wilde, Williams, Wolfe, Yeats. I walked back and pulled a copy of Ginsberg poetry from the shelf. It was a signed first edition. The collected poems of Edgar Allan Poe caught my eye. I reached for the volume and gently opened it.

"Take this kiss upon the brow!/And in parting from you now/Thus much let me avow—/All that we see or seem/Is but a dream within a dream."

I practically jumped into the bookcase. McGowan stood just inches behind me, quoting Poe in a stentorian voice. I turned around and looked up into his smug face. "You scared the shit out of me," I said.

He grabbed my shoulders and pressed his lips firmly to my forehead. "There's a goddamn lunatic holed up in a tract house on the north side. I'm backup on special enforcement detail."

"What does that entail, exactly?"

"It means I now get to put on my bulletproof vest and try to keep the television crews at bay."

"While you're doing that I'm going to go home and take a

bubble bath," I said. "Before we part, though, did you ever get the address of the scraggly guy who owned the car that veered into Janice's?"

"Yeah. I left it on your machine earlier this evening."

"What did you say the guy's name was?"

"Rob. Rob Drum. The name should be easy to remember—it rhymes with scum. I even brought home a copy of the updated accident report for you."

The accident report was sitting on a table in the front hall. McGowan handed it to me, then rummaged in the hall closet. He emerged holding a black knapsack. "My Superman vest," he explained. We wasted no time getting to our respective cars. As I started my engine he pulled his car alongside mine and we rolled down our windows.

"Sweet dreams within your dreams," I said.

"And miles to go before I sleep," he answered.

16

It was late. The witching hour, I mused. Suitable for sorcery and supernatural occurrences. The only wizardry I was up to at the moment was the deciphering of a badly written police report. I sat on the sofa, legs outstretched, my skin still warm and fragrant from the bath. Whitman seemed to appreciate this, as he'd parked himself between my thighs. Cats, too, can be direct.

The report was disappointing. The alleged owner of the other car in Janice's accident, Rob Rhymes-with-Scum Drum, had helped the cops fill in some of the blanks, but not many. He'd told them the "acquaintance" who'd borrowed his car the night of the accident was named Michael Huerte, and he'd positively identified Huerte's three-day-old corpse at the county morgue. The victim purportedly had a brother somewhere in East L.A., but the LAPD had been unable to locate said brother. Reading between the lines of the report, I gathered they'd stopped trying.

Señor Huerte, you see, was not a U.S. citizen. He had no Social Security number, no credit history, no military record. There was a notation in the report that Huerte was rumored to have more family somewhere south of the border, "whereabouts unknown." Huerte's body had been relegated to a cut-rate funeral parlor and the state had picked up the tab. A photocopy of the billing was attached.

That was about all I could glean from the police paperwork. The narrative section was handwritten in neat capital letters, but the facts were sketchy and awkwardly worded. It said nothing to indicate that anyone had asked Rob Drum *why* he'd allowed Señor Huerte to borrow his car. Not that Drum would have necessarily told the truth. Only Huerte's intoxicated corpse had been found in the wreck. There were no drugs under the seats, no bodies in the trunk, so I guess the cops saw no point in further inquiry. To me the fact that Rob Drum had been more upset about his car being totaled than his acquaintance being dead hit a sour note. And if you didn't know an undocumented alien that well, why on earth would you let him borrow your car?

I intended to find out. I was raring to find out. But it was late, and most of the civilized world was asleep. I needed something to dull my senses, to put me out. I got up and turned on the TV. It's about the only thing I can think of that TV is good for.

A woman wearing too much makeup, even for the TV cameras, appeared on the screen. She was bursting with enthusiasm about a secret that had transformed her life: a consultation with one of the world's most famous psychics, Lenny Lenton. In fact, Lenny would be appearing on the show a little later ("So don't go away!"). They would be showing an actual videotape of one of Lenny's readings, she promised breathlessly. At this point a cut from the videotape appeared. One of Lenny's bedazzled clients, tears running down her cheeks, was saying, "Lenny, you're so amazing! How can I ever thank you?" A 900 number flashed on the screen and the voiceover announced that Lenny's hand-picked psychics were on the line, waiting to talk to you *now*.

I put my face in my hands and groaned.

When I looked up the madeup woman was interviewing Lenny's readers, the chosen ones. She was pointing out to the viewers at home that Lenny's select psychics were all very "positive people." I began to get a funny feeling in the pit of my stomach. I picked up the phone and dialed Linda. It didn't matter that it was 12:42 A.M. After all, Linda was a witch, too.

"Hel-lo," her pleasant voice answered.

"I'm watching this Lenny Lenton thing," I said.

"The infomercial?"

"I guess so. This isn't the outfit you're working for, is it? Tell me it's not."

Silence.

"Linda, my God. These people are surreal. They look like they eat Pat Boone tapes for breakfast."

Much giggling. "They probably do!" More giggling.

Linda is one of my best friends. Whereas my gift is best characterized by sporadic clairvoyance, Linda is almost always on. She is highly intuitive about people and consistently accurate. Her insights tend to be healing. Several months ago she quit her job marketing computer software and signed on with a psychic hotline.

"I can't believe you can do this job," I said. "How can you?"

"I couldn't stand another day of wearing panty hose," she said. I understood completely.

"But what do you say if your gift fails you? Do you just make stuff up?"

"You'd be surprised. It doesn't take psychic ability to help most of these callers. You want to know a typical call? I get this one about twelve times a day: 'Now I know my man drinks, and sometimes he beats me, but I *love* him, I really do. He disappeared with my welfare check this week. I know he's been seein' another woman . . . but, um, can you tell me when he's comin' back?'"

"That's sad," I said.

"I know. I try to send as many of them as I can to Al-Anon."

"So what about your coworkers at the hotline? Are they all as reasonable as you?"

"Are you kidding? Most of them are certifiable. In all fairness, though, the place has a few really talented readers. It's like any other job, in a lot of ways. The shit here definitely floats to the top. The owner has already served one sentence for embezzlement. Those of us who work with him have no reason to believe he won't serve another."

"The infomercial is a disgrace. You know that."

"Lord, yes. By the way, my dear, while we're on the subject of readings, I see a man around you."

I glanced around the living room. "Oh, yeah? Where?"

"Someone special is occupying your thoughts. Come on, tell me who he is."

"Linda, there is no man in my life. Your job is making you nutsoid."

"Liar. He's in the military—no, he's a police officer, isn't he?"

"If I tell you will you help me with the murder case I'm working on?"

"Deal."

"His name is Tom, he kissed me on the forehead, and that's all there is to tell. Now, does the name Janice Freeman conjure up any images in particular?"

"There will be more of this Tom person."

"Janice Freeman."

"Oh, all right. Blonde hair? Attractive?"

"Yes."

"I don't get a good feeling."

"You wouldn't. She's dead."

Linda was silent for a long time. "I don't get a good feeling about *you*, Elizabeth," she said slowly. "This Janice Freeman business is dangerous."

"Do you get any sense of why it's dangerous? Names, places, images, anything?"

Linda made a distressed sound. "Augh! I can't do this, Liz. I'm not kidding. I'm frightened for you."

The infomercial was wrapping up. I turned up the sound.

"Here," I said to Linda. "This ought to straighten you out." I held the mouthpiece of the phone up to the TV, where the madeup lady was speaking earnestly into the camera.

". . . Most of all, I learned from Lenny that no matter how bad things might seem, there is always a *reason* for the experience we're going through. And that with a positive attitude, anything, even your *wildest dreams*, can and will come true!" Schmaltzy music began to play and the 900 number zoomed from right to left across the bottom of the screen. I pulled the phone back from the flickering television.

"Are you still there?" I asked.

I heard laughter on the line. "It's a paycheck," Linda said.

"Has anyone ever accused you of being weird?"

"Has anyone not?"

"I'm so glad you're my friend," I said.

"Aw, shucks. Me, too. I mean, you too. I mean—"

"I know what you mean."

17

Rob Drum lived in Pacific Beach, a popular community along the southern shore of San Diego. Especially in the summer, thousands of tourists like live sardines squeeze in and out of the colorful beachside boutiques, giving PB a certain hustling charm during the day. But when the crowds mill out at sunset, the town can turn ugly. A vagrant population has staked out this stretch of beach, preying on unsuspecting nighttime visitors and careless residents. The area is one of the hot spots on the San Diego crime report, and the place has broken its own record in volume of burglaries for the last five consecutive years.

I awoke early the next morning, knowing I'd better get to Pacific Beach before the surf was up. I thought it would be prudent to don the native dress. I rummaged through my storage closet and came up with the top half of an old bikini and a shredded pair of cutoff jeans. While digging through some boxes I happened upon a pair of hoop earrings the size of bracelets that a well-meaning friend had given me several years ago. I dragged the whole getup into the bathroom and watched as piece by piece I transformed myself into a beach babe. I added frosted hot pink lipstick and let my hair hang loosely around my face. Checking out the total effect in the three-way mirror, I noticed that my butt cheeks were hanging out of the cutoffs a bit, which was perfect. I just hoped I wouldn't bump into anyone I knew.

Ordinarily this time of year the warming air meets the cold Pacific and the coast becomes shrouded in fog—what the meteorologists call the marine layer. Their television counterparts refer to the phenomenon as "night and morning low clouds," but the rest of us call it June gloom. This particular summer had been bizarre, though, full of uncommon weather conditions. We'd had thunderstorms and high humidity, which were practically unheard of in San Diego. Word was that we'd been visited upon by El Niño, the warm current that sometimes kicks up from southern latitudes, bringing with it the moods of the tropics. I stepped out the door and into the heat of a sunlit sauna, and it was only eight o'clock in the morning. My scanty garb was beginning to seem sensible, after all.

The address McGowan had given me for Rob Drum was 1166 ½ Santa Cruz Avenue. I knew roughly where that was. Santa Cruz ran parallel to the coastline, just two blocks from the water's edge. I pulled off the Pacific Beach exit and impatiently made my way west through a maddening number of traffic lights. I truly admire those people who can mosey nonchalantly through heavy traffic, not caring whether the lights turn green or red. Me, I like to *move*.

I reached Santa Cruz Avenue and turned south. The lights turned to stop signs at every corner and traffic slowed to a queue, inching along in a start-and-stop manner like some loosely linked worm. Parked cars flanked both sides of the avenue, leaving the narrowest of passageways. Pedestrians swarmed down the sidewalks, dashing in and out through the parked cars and across the line of traffic.

At this pace there was nothing to do but see sights. The avenue was lined with shops selling up-to-the-nanosecond surf styles—the coolest shorts, T-shirts, and sandals on the planet. Skateboarders weaved expertly among the tourists, hopping curbs without a care. Everything seemed to shout with color, including the faces, arms, and backs of the locals, which glowed with ruddy suntans.

Without warning I witnessed a miracle. A black Datsun 240ZX parked just ahead on my right indicated with a left turn signal that it desired to vacate its space. Kindly I obliged, then whipped into that gap like white on rice. I had two blocks to go before reaching Rob Drum's address, but I hadn't seen a parking space in the last half mile. Besides, I figured, at this crawl I'd get there faster hoofing it, anyway.

I found the eleven hundred block and spent several minutes trying to deduce where the heck 1166 ½ would be. There was, sure enough, an 1166—Dinko's Frozen Yogurt—and directly adjacent, an 1168—Pia Mia's, a tiny boutique selling custom-made bikinis. After several minutes of hanging out on the sidewalk, pretending to be making up my mind about whether to pig out or try on a bathing suit, I went into the yogurt shop to ask for help.

A teenage girl wearing a blonde ponytail and a yellow apron stitched with the "Dinko's" logo was filling one of the condiment bins behind the counter with carob-covered raisins.

"Excuse me, can you tell me where I'd find eleven sixty-six and a half Santa Cruz Avenue?" I asked.

"Uh . . . oh! This is it," she said with a vacuous smile, "eleven sixty-six."

"No, I'm looking for eleven sixty-six *and a half*."

She frowned hard, like this was the strangest question she'd ever heard. "I don't know!" she exclaimed. "Sorry!" She grinned at me as if that would be the best news I'd hear all day.

I had better luck in the bikini shop. As I walked through the door a ribbon of small bells on the door jamb shimmered like cymbals. A dark beauty of about forty approached from the rear of the shop. A curtain of thick brown hair hung to her narrow waist and all but obscured the tiny purple bra top she wore. Her hips were tightly wrapped in an exotic orange and purple sarong that just grazed her ankles.

"Hello," she said warmly. Her voice was deep, with a mu-

sical quality that made me think of cellos and civilized eve-
nings at the symphony.

I was suddenly self-conscious about the stretched and
faded bikini top I wore, a remnant from my college days.
Not to mention the ridiculous earrings and slutty cutoffs. I
wanted to say, "I know I look like shit but believe it or not I
dressed this way deliberately. Undercover work and all." Instead I said, "You look beautiful. Do you think something
like that"—I pointed to her outfit—"would work on me?"

She assessed me with large cocoa colored eyes, and I
could see her mind working. "Not this. But I have a suit that
was just made for you. Come here."

I followed her through the swimsuit racks toward the
back of the shop, captivated by her graceful walk. "Wait
here," she said, disappearing through a pair of swinging
doors.

She reappeared carrying an armful of cobalt blue fabric.
There were three pieces—a top and bottom made of spandex and a tunic in the same shade but constructed of something incredibly light and sheer. Rob Drum, I decided,
would just have to wait a few minutes.

"The dressing room is right over here. Let me know if you
need any help. My name is Pia."

"Thanks, Pia."

In the dressing room, the bathing suit fit like a second
skin. I slipped the tunic over the suit. It was soft and see-
through, the blue as deep and brilliant as precious stones.
"Hey," I called out, "this is great."

"I'd love to see it on you," Pia called back.

Her face lit up as she watched me come out of the dressing room. "That's exactly how I dreamed it would look
when I designed it," she said, examining the outfit with a
practiced eye.

"You designed this?"

She nodded and indicated with a twirling finger for me to

turn around. I rotated obediently. "Very nice. Let's see it without the cover-up," she said.

I unsashed the sheer thing and let it fall from my shoulders. Pia was shaking her head from side to side but still smiling proudly, I was relieved to see. "I can't believe how perfect that is on you," she said.

"It sure is more comfortable than my old suit."

"You needed more support on top," she said matter-of-factly. She caught my embarrassed look and added emphatically, "I would love to be able to wear a top like that. You have an exquisite figure, really."

"Thanks." Exquisite? I tried to let the compliment sink in. I'd been a gangly adolescent. Years ago the relentless teasing of eighth-grade boys brainwashed me into conceiving of myself as a flat-chested eyesore. I continue to work hard at deprogramming.

After wearing Pia's creations, getting back into the things I'd had on felt like dressing from a garbage can. I couldn't find price tags on any of her pieces and I didn't ask. You might find a suit like this once every other lifetime.

I took the outfit to the cash register and spent several seconds searching my purse for my wallet, a process that required me to empty half the contents onto the counter. "Purse organization is definitely not my strong suit," I said, handing Pia my VISA card.

"Hardly a fatal character flaw," she answered with a smile. "Is there anything else I can help you with today?"

"Actually, there is. Is there such a thing as eleven sixty-six and a half Santa Cruz Avenue?"

A displeased expression crossed her face. "Unfortunately, yes," she said slowly as she swiped my card and waited for the purchase to clear. "This shop is on a double lot. Eleven sixty-six and a half is the dump in back." She looked up, one brow arched with interest. "You're not looking to buy the place, are you?"

The computer approved the purchase and began to print the receipt with a grinding staccato. "No, I just need to talk to a guy named Rob Drum. Do you know him?"

"No, I don't know any of them back there," she answered disdainfully. "Not that it's any of my business, but these are not people you want to know." She gave me the charge slip and a ballpoint pen. As she handed my VISA card back she quickly glanced at it. "Elizabeth Chase. Well, well. Nice to meet you, Elizabeth."

"The pleasure is mine," I said. "Now, may I ask a favor?"

"Sure."

"Would you give me a call if you do find out anything about this Rob Drum guy?"

She nodded. I wrote my phone number on one of the Pacific Properties brochures I'd pulled from my purse and handed it across the counter to her. Then I signed my name to the charge slip, added ten dollars to the total and returned the receipt. "Pia, you're very kind, you're an excellent designer, and you don't ask enough for your lovely creations! I would have been willing to pay twice what you charged me for that."

"Just tell people where you got it," she laughed.

"Sure will. I'll be back myself."

I had nearly reached the door when she called out, "Elizabeth, wait!" She scurried toward me and pressed something into my palm. "Wear these with the new suit, okay?"

I opened my hand to find a pair of deep blue earrings, classic rounds of lapis lazuli. Several legends, I knew, clung to the semiprecious stone. In ancient Egypt lapis was worn to protect against evil spirits and mishaps. Wearing lapis, the ancients believed, gave one access to an inexhaustible and holy power. In Christian folklore, lapis is said to have fallen from the crown of Lucifer as he was banished from heaven, and it remains in the keeping of the holy angels.

I stood staring at the blue earrings for several seconds, contemplating these things and also the fact that they were a darn good match with the bathing suit. When I looked up Pia's deep eyes were glowing at me. I tried to think of proper words of gratitude.

"Thank you. I think I needed these," I said at last.

18

It's rumored among those who know me that my purse can hold a kitchen sink. That's not quite true, although I suppose it's roomy enough for at least a couple of place settings. I took the multicolored Pia Mia's bag holding my new outfit and stashed it in my trusty purse with plenty of room to spare. No point in taking the trouble to dress like a native and then carry around a shopping bag that shouts, "Tourista!" That handled, I popped a stick of gum into my mouth and wandered around the side of the shop, looking for a way into the back lot.

There was a space about four feet wide between Pia Mia's and the next store over. I walked between the two buildings and into an unkempt back lot. A freestanding wooden structure, the humble kind of bungalow you see advertised as granny's quarters, stood forlornly among the weeds. There was no driveway per se—it looked as if the main access to the bungalow was from an alley in the rear. As I approached I could hear the muffled throbbing of a stereo blasting inside.

Not finding a doorbell, I knocked forcefully. The door opened and a deafening roar of drums and electric guitars flooded into the thick summer air. A man wearing camouflage parachute pants and no shirt stared down at me through half-open eyelids. Long blond hair streamed over his bare shoulders.

"Hi!" I yelled over the din.

" 'Lo." I could hardly hear his soft, stoner voice.

I knew if I asked for Rob Rhymes-with-Scum Drum there was an outside chance that this person, whoever he was, would connect me with the recent accident—and the police. I pretended to be looking for Michael Huerte instead.

"Have you seen Michael around here anywhere!" I asked, raising my voice above the music.

"I dunno, just a sec." He mumbled so that all the words seemed to run together.

The half-naked guy hadn't exactly offered an invitation, but I stepped in after him and let the door shut behind me. The noise pounding through the place was a prime example of heavy metal at its worst: screaming guitars, relentless drums, and painfully loud bass, each instrument playing to a different beat. The overall effect was like a truckload of china hitting a cement wall. I glanced at my watch: 9:15 A.M. These guys were neighbors from Hades, all right.

I found myself standing in a kitchen that could belong only to bachelors. A majority of the cabinet doors were hanging open, and the shelves were nearly empty. Most of the dishware was piled onto the counters and filled the small sink. Out of all of it, not two pieces appeared to match. Some clever lad had performed an impromptu papering of the walls with the dregs of bumper-sticker philosophy. I took a few moments to scan the messages: YOU'VE OBVIOUSLY MISTAKEN ME FOR SOMEONE WHO CARES. DIAL 911/MAKE A COP COME. I'D SMACK YOU BUT SHIT SPLATTERS—these were just a few of the charmers that caught my eye. The pièce de résistance had been given top billing above the door: I MAY NOT GO DOWN IN HISTORY—BUT I'LL GO DOWN ON YOUR DAUGHTER.

The music came to a sudden frenzied, banging conclusion and for a moment there was blessed silence. I had no sooner breathed a sigh of relief when it cranked back up again. I suffered through an entire song that sounded essentially the same as the last one, with the addition of an angry, screeching vocal part. At last I had to conclude I'd been forgotten.

Tentatively, I wandered out of the kitchen and into a small living room area. Here, too, the walls had been papered, this time with a lively assortment of posters whose themes ran to cars, female flesh, and black leather. Hanging above an old television—the focal point of the room—was a white flag featuring a large black swastika.

Half a dozen guys were hanging out. The lot of them looked about one step up from the streets. Three were draped on a shabby, misshapen sofa, silently drinking beer from long-necked brown bottles. The other three were sitting on the floor playing cards and carrying on a halfhearted argument about who dealt last. I didn't see the blond who'd answered the door.

My appearance didn't create much of a stir. One of the long-haired cardplayers looked up at me and nodded, then went back to inspecting the hand he'd been dealt. For several seconds I stood there wondering what to say. Finally one of the guys on the sofa spotted me and hopped to his feet. He shoved his hands into the pockets of his jeans and sauntered over.

I tried to remember when I'd last seen so much hair. He wore a thick beard and mustache, but they were no match for his outrageous mane of frizzy brown. The hair seemed to have a personality all its own, an aggressive one at that.

As he came closer I was able to make out the person inside all the fuzz. He was petite but excessively muscular. His pectoral muscles pushed out the eagle wings emblazoned across the chest of his black Harley-Davidson T-shirt, and the sleeves were filled to bulging with biceps and triceps. As a whole, his face was not unattractive. His features were sharp and symmetrical, his eyes thickly lashed and shiny black-brown. Yet something in the little man's visage disturbed me. If you were to meet the evil gnome guarding the bridge that was your only escape from a Gothic nightmare, this would be the guy.

"Hi!" he said in an oily, overfriendly voice. He wiggled his eyebrows and stared straight at my chest.

Inwardly, I cringed. Outwardly, I smiled, chewed my gum, and yelled over the relentless head-banging metal, "Hi! Have you seen Michael around?"

A troubled look came into his wizened little features. "Michael Huerte?" he yelled back.

"Yeah!" I yelled, nodding enthusiastically. "He told me I might catch him here!"

He walked over to the stereo and the music ended abruptly as he punched the stop button. "Hey!" one of the cardplayers yelled angrily.

"Just a second, asshole!" the gnome snarled. He walked back over to me, eyeballing my crotch while he was at it. "Um, I hate to tell you this," he said as he shoved his hands into his pockets, "but Michael has passed on." I didn't feel any sympathy or sadness on his part, just a thin effort to state the facts in what would pass as a civilized manner. "Were you a friend of his?" he asked.

The dumbfounded expression on my face was genuine. No matter how many times I'd seen it, this kind of coldness amazed me. "Yes, I was," I answered. Being a friend of mankind, I didn't feel this was a lie. Not entirely, anyway.

"What—what happened?" I stammered.

The guys on the floor had stopped their card game to eavesdrop, and now they all spoke at once. "He was in a car crash, man . . . yeah, it was gnarly . . . he was totally wasted, man . . . car was totaled . . . it was heavy, man . . . . Rob was really bummed—"

They referred here to Rob Drum, no doubt. "Rob?" I asked. "Who's Rob?"

"Rob was unfortunate enough to have lent Mike his car that night," said the gnome. His eyes glittered and the corners of his mouth turned up, as if he found that quite funny. I noticed a slight Poindexter tone in his voice, a touch too much intelligence. I wondered if perhaps he'd been a rejected nerd in high school and this renegade debauchery was his way of fighting back.

"So does this guy Rob know exactly what happened? I mean, can I talk to him?" I asked.

"Um, he's in the other room, probably getting loaded." The gnome stared right through what little clothes I had on, smiling lewdly. With exaggerated hospitality he asked, "Would you like a beer?" So thoughtful, such a host.

"No thanks," I said. "God, poor Michael."

I was doing my best to play the bereaved airhead here. I hoped I was pulling it off. These people weren't responding to the situation the way normal human beings would, and their lack of humanity was throwing me off. This was one of those crowds in which any display of emotion—with the possible exception of anger—definitely wasn't cool.

"So does anybody know how it happened?" I asked. "Where was he going, do you know?"

"Who knows?" the gnome answered. "They probably borrowed the car to go party."

One of the guys sitting on the floor nodded at me. He was still holding five cards in his hand, but carelessly so that his measly pair of fours was in plain view. "Yeah, fucking drunk driving," he piped in. "What's a bummer, man, is Michael didn't even drink."

The kid sitting next to him quipped: "Hey, I don't think he even knew how to *drive!*"

The third guy swilled his beer and joked, "Wull, apparently *not!*" At that the gang broke into uproarious laughter, a couple of them falling over backward.

Another voice rose above the hilarity. "Hey, shitheads! Calling all degenerates!" The words issued from a man who appeared in the doorway at the back of the room. With his uncombed hair and lined face, he was scraggly enough to fit

McGowan's description of Rob Drum. But then all these gentlemen were excellent candidates. The blond who'd answered the door stood silently behind him. "I hate to break this up, but we've got to crash, man. See you guys later, okay?"

His direct gaze included me in the group that had just been invited to leave, which I considered a blessing. There was certainly more I could find out here, but I wasn't willing to pay the price. I turned to walk out.

"Hey, *you* don't have to leave," the gnome said, grabbing my arm. He pulled me close enough that his frizzy hair grazed my cheek. In a hushed voice he said into my ear, "These guys have been partying here for two days. We just want to get rid of them, you know?" His acrid beer breath filled my nostrils, and out of the corner of my eye I could see him staring down my cleavage.

"Thanks anyway, but I've got work to do," I said, heading for the door.

One of the cardplayers overheard my last comment. He made a disgusted face and said, "Eww! Work!" The party was breaking up and the small crowd milling out of the living room started laughing.

"You have a *job?*" The gnome smiled but wrinkled his nose with contempt. "I feel so sorry for you."

I was aching to turn back and say, "The feelings are genuinely mutual," but I kept my closing remarks to a minimum. "See ya," I said.

19

I was feeling nauseated. I couldn't get the gnome's beer breath out of my nostrils. Not only that, I could still hear the ungodly heavy metal playing in my memory as I walked the two blocks back to my car. An artery in my left temple picked up the beat, throbbing oppressively. I wanted to think about what I'd just witnessed, but my nausea and my headache, combined with the heat and the humidity, made it difficult to focus. Halfway to my car I decided to forget about work for a while and go to the ocean, as long as I was this close. I headed due west, past the boulevard of tourist traps along the coast. I found access to the beach through an alley bisecting a row of funky mismatched houses lining the sand.

I stopped into a cement-block outbuilding that served as the beach's public restroom and changed into my new bathing suit. The color had been vibrant in Pia's shop, but here in the sunlight it practically pulsated with an otherworldly blue. The ephemeral color brought to mind the lapis lazuli earrings. I pulled them from my purse and once again held them in my palm. The blue stones were heavy for their size; they had an integrity wholly absent from ersatz costume jewelry. I put them on and couldn't deny feeling oddly empowered.

I headed north along the beach, away from the hubbub of the southern shore. In this direction, I knew, the crowds would thin to a core of locals. I walked the border between two elements, where water met earth. The day's towering white clouds were reflected in the thin sheet of shimmering ocean at my feet. As I stepped along the mirrored sand I looked down at the clouds and pretended I was walking through the sky. The wind whipped through my hair and cooled my scalp. The muffled crashing of the waves, rhythmic and comforting, eased the tension in my temples. Soon the memory of the jarring stereo faded. My stomach relaxed and I was able to breathe deeply again.

I had no beach blanket, but I staked my terrain all the same. The top layer of sand was hot from the sun, so I dug a cool rectangular demigrave about two inches deep. I lowered my body and found the patch of sand surprisingly sensual in a damp, grainy kind of way. I had half a notion to growl and roll in it.

I'm not one for long periods of inactivity. I soon sat up to fish in my purse for reading material. One of the reasons I cart around a handbag the size of carry-on luggage is so I can accommodate a book or two. That way if I'm ever stuck waiting in line or for an appointment, I can fall into the wonderful worlds created by authors, rather than bitching, pacing, and raising my heart rate. Patience is not one of my virtues, and you have to know how to manage your character defects. Too bad I can't read in heavy traffic.

As I was plumbing the unknown depths of my handbag I began to have the uncomfortable feeling I was being watched. I quickly rationalized that I couldn't wear an electric blue bathing suit on a relatively empty beach and expect not to be noticed. Casually, I turned around and looked back toward land. There were relatively few beachgoers, about what you'd expect at ten-thirty in the morning on a weekday. A young mother was hoisting an umbrella to shade her toddler, who was raucously babbling in a portable playpen. A man and woman, sunny sides up, glistened nut brown and oily about twenty feet over. A couple of joggers were puffing along the water's edge. The only person who seemed to be watching anything was the lifeguard perched on his tower, staring out to sea through binoculars.

I shrugged off the feeling and resumed my search for reading material. The first things I fished out were the slippery brochures Janice Freeman's boss had given me yesterday. The technicolor photos depicted impossibly perfect properties: no telephone wires, no smog in the sky, no clouds in the sky for that matter. The brochures basically told the same story Stan had given me: Pacific Properties owned a gagillion places that generated a gagillion dollars. The implication was that if you didn't invest you just didn't care about making easy money with no risk whatsoever to your original investment.

My eyes wandered over to a little snack bar by the lifeguard tower. A hand-painted sign advertised frozen bananas and mangoes-on-a-stick. I pulled myself to my feet and walked over, feeling eyes on me the entire way. I found this sensation of being scrutinized by complete strangers extremely unnerving. It occurred to me that actresses and models have to put up with this all the time. I wondered how they could stand it.

Then something I noticed near the rear of the snack bar spoiled everything: a public telephone. Coming to the beach had been my willful attempt to play hooky from my investigation for a while. But the appearance of this telephone struck me as a tenacious mountain moving to a reluctant Mohammed. After all, I did have three phone calls to make.

First, I put a call in to Mom, who was out. I asked her via tape recording if she would please consult her vast resources for Pacific Properties's financial history and get back to me if she found anything condemning.

Next I pulled from my purse the envelope Alan had given me in Denny's parking lot last night. I called the number he'd written in a shaking hand. Alan's voice—unclouded by grief—came on the line, confidently informing me that he was not home, but that if I'd leave a message he'd be happy to call back. Again I spoke on tape, reminding him who I was and that I'd like to get together again to discuss Janice's accident if he felt up to it.

Finally I put a call in to the Escondido Police Department. McGowan was at his desk and the receptionist put the call right through.

I greeted him with a question. "So how many miles did you actually go before you slept last night?"

"I measure the distance in Styrofoam cups of coffee. Too many. The shrinks finally coaxed the asshole out at about four this morning. How about you? Any interesting dreams within your dreams?"

"I can't remember. The alarm woke me up and scared all my dreams away. Except for this one, of course."

Silence.

"Tom? You there?"

"Sorry. I'm a little slow on the draw today. Sleep deprivation."

"I'll make this short, then. I just visited the address you gave me for Rob Drum—"

"Rhymes with scum, yeah, I remember—"

"No kidding. There was a whole nest of vermin at that place. What did you say Rob Drum looked like?"

"Long hair, brown, scraggly—your basic lowlife."

"That description fits about all of them."

"So what'd you find out?"

"I don't know, I'm just sorting it out. I counted eight guys either drinking beer or getting high—at nine in the morning, no less. They basically verified the story Drum gave you about Michael Huerte borrowing his car. But something one of the guys said is bugging me."

"What's that?"

"Well, this might not be anything, but he said it was a shame about the accident because Michael Huerte didn't even drink."

"He did a good job of it that night," Tom replied. "His blood alcohol was three times the limit."

"I know, but I just keep thinking. Going on our assumption that the accident was a setup, someone like Michael Huerte—a foreigner who'd leave no paper trail, no family—would be a perfect sitting duck."

There was silence on the other end, so I went on. "And another thing. When I asked where they thought Michael had been going, one of the guys answered, 'They probably went to go party.' Not 'he,' Tom—'*they*.' Yet Michael Huerte was the only one in the car at the time of the accident. It all fits, you know? Huerte left with someone but died alone."

"Let's go out there," McGowan said.

"Out where?"

"To the accident site. I'm out of here at five today, so I can meet you on Del Dios about a quarter after. Just look for my car along the side of the road, about five miles in."

"You sure you want to go those extra miles before you sleep? You sound utterly beat."

Silence.

"Tom?"

"No, I'll be fine." He was mumbling. "I'm going to take a little nap right now."

"Okay. But maybe you'd better hang up the phone first."

Silence.

"Tom?"

Silence.

"Tom?"

More silence. Then: "Just teasing you. See you at five."

I opted for the mango-on-a-stick and carried it back to my spot on the sand. I felt a sharp pang of disappointment as I bit through the firm, coral-colored skin—the fruit wasn't quite ripe. Damn it all, I was doing my best to luxuriate in this brief vacation here at the beach, but the whole day was tasting sour somehow.

I pulled out a paperback and read for a couple of hours before I eventually nodded off. I dozed in fits and starts, the sounds of the seaside occasionally penetrating my trancelike napping. Gradually I fell into a genuinely deep sleep.

I don't know how long I'd been out when I woke up with a start. I had been dreaming something I felt an urgency to remember, but the screech of a seagull had jerked me back to consciousness and jarred the imagery from my mind. I opened my eyes to find the creature bouncing, wings outstretched, just a few feet from my head. The bird's steel gray eyes were intent on the meaty remains of my mango. An old boyfriend had called these gulls "sea rats," which didn't seem far off at the moment.

"Get out of here," I said, waving the gull away.

The voice was so near that for a moment I had the irrational thought the gull itself had answered me.

"Creepy things, aren't they?" it said.

20

The words had come from behind me. The gull stood its ground to my right. Unless this bird could throw a human voice, I had company. Slowly, I turned around.

From sand level, the first thing I saw was the curly leg hair coming through the lavish rips in his jeans. I was disoriented from my nap, and the hirsute legs made for a rude and repulsive awakening. The gnome was sitting cross-legged directly behind me. From the grin on his face, he was enjoying the view.

"Fancy meeting me here, huh?" he said.

I didn't feel like chatting. I guess I was kind of hoping this was a dream within a dream, and that it would go away.

"I thought you said you had a *job*," he continued. His voice wasn't just snide, it was mean. "Somebody *pay* you to sleep on the beach? Even I could handle that job."

My head was finally beginning to clear. I felt more dreadful with each passing moment. I groaned under my breath.

"So what *do* you do, anyway?" he sneered.

Nope, he wasn't going to go away. I sat up and gave him a dirty look. The words "get the fuck out of here" were on the tip of my tongue, but I thought it best not to provoke him with naughty language.

"What *do* you do?" he repeated.

"I'm a snake charmer," I replied.

He reached into his pocket and pulled out a joint. "You

want to get stoned?" My second offer so far this week. He stoked it up with a Bic lighter without waiting for my reply. I wondered if he ever caught his frizzy hair on fire doing that. When he held the joint out for me I shook my head.

"So what's your name?" I said.

He looked at me like I was crazy. "My *name?*" He chuckled, a tight nasal sound with no mirth in it. "Let's see. What's my name." He took another hit off the joint, held it in his lungs, and stared intently down the shoreline. A few seconds later he exhaled. "How about Bob?" He nodded his head slightly, still squinting into the southern horizon. "Yeah, that's a good one. Bob." He turned his dark, shiny eyes on me. They were filled with fuck-you cynicism.

"You don't look like a Bob," I said.

"You don't look much like a snake charmer, either."

A skirmish erupted nearby. The gull, attempting to drag away the mango remains, had attracted the competition of his peers. There was much screeching and flapping of wings.

"So," said the gnome, "you were a friend of Huerte's. Were you fucking him, too?" Anger flashed in his eyes. He pitched the rest of the joint at the sand near my feet.

"I beg your pardon?"

" 'I beg your pardon?' " he mimicked. His imitation of my self-controlled modulation was perfect. " 'I *beg* your pardon.' I like that. Ooo, yeah, honey, beg me."

I'd had enough. I got to my feet, grabbed my purse, and started walking.

"You know, you're not very friendly," he called after me.

I stepped along swiftly. From a distance the sound of his cheerless laughter blended eerily with the screeching of the gulls.

21

A queue of cars trailed me as I drove the winding miles along Del Dios. I felt pressured and a bit nerve-racked. I could sense the drivers behind me urging me to speed up, and I empathized with their frustration. It wouldn't do to go any faster, though. I was anxiously searching the side of the road and didn't want to pass Tom's police cruiser should it suddenly appear behind one of the sharp bends. No telling when I'd find another place to turn around.

Finally I spotted him. I signaled and pumped my brakes to alert the driver behind me, then turned off onto the dirt shoulder, where there was just enough room to pull in and brake sharply behind the cruiser. I let out a sigh and only then realized I'd been holding my breath. There was no guard rail here, and this cliff was no gentle slope—it was a sheer drop. A red Toyota pickup and a beat-up gray Subaru pulled past me impatiently. I didn't blame them.

McGowan was leaning against the driver's side of his vehicle, arms folded across his chest. He scowled at me as I got out of my car.

"You're a traffic hazard in that thing," he said. At first I thought he was referring to my driving. Then he added, "But it sure is a great color on you," and I realized he was talking about my bathing suit. I had pulled the cutoffs back on and had hoped the see-through tunic would suffice for a shirt. It had to.

"Don't think I haven't felt self-conscious all day, okay? I didn't have time to go home and change." I hate being cranky like this. McGowan didn't deserve it.

"Believe me, I'm not complaining," he said gently.

"So this is the spot, huh?" I tried to sound friendly and businesslike.

"Actually, it's a few yards beyond here, but this was the only turnoff where it seemed safe to park."

We walked along the narrow, gravelly ridge between the paved road and the sage-covered cliff. I walked behind McGowan, excruciatingly aware of the flesh visible at the tops of my thighs. For the umpteenth time that day, I regretted the damn cutoffs. Sure enough, it wasn't two minutes before some hormone-crazed kid leaned out his window and let out a loud, embarrassing catcall.

"Oh, for crying out loud," I said.

McGowan turned around, a frown on his face. "He's a beast, a brute, a barbarian, a savage. An animal. A Neanderthal."

I nodded heartily, pleased with the assessment.

"Of course, he expressed my sentiments exactly," McGowan added.

I made no comment but pondered deeply on why a comment that would offend me coming from someone else felt like a compliment coming from Tom. Probably because I lusted after him, too. Ah, the capricious and confusing social mores of the 1990s. I felt sorry for men these days.

We walked another hundred feet and McGowan stopped. "This is it."

We stood silently for a few moments, taking our respective inventories. McGowan looked out over the drop where Janice had left this world. He knit his brows and cocked his head slightly to the side, as if he were listening for an answer. I stood on the narrow ledge and watched the oncoming cars veer toward us around the bend, their tires humming with centrifugal force. Headlights turned into wide-open eyes and front-end grilles grimaced with the danger and strain of the climb.

I walked to the edge of the cliff and looked down. I didn't recognize the spot, not from this viewpoint. I looked across the highway. On the opposite side of the road a driveway climbed to the very top of the mountainside.

"Tom," I said, tapping his shoulder. He turned around and I pointed to the driveway across the street. "What do you think?"

"If someone were to set up an accident, that would be an ideal place to roll a car into oncoming traffic," he said.

We looked both ways and dashed across the road. The driveway led steeply up the side of the mountain, and making the climb was no small effort. It led to a newly graded pad, where we stood and caught our breath. Del Dios Drive, snaking below, was in plain view from this elevation. The two curves that would be blind from road level could be seen clearly from here.

I expected to feel a flash of recognition, or a sense of déjà vu. But the sun bathed the entire scene in glorious light and color, and it bore practically no resemblance to the place I'd visited astrally. I thought back to the night of my vision and tried to regain the scene. I remembered the contents of what I'd witnessed: From high above, a road. Two men. A car. But there was no immediacy to the memory. The images were as dusty and lifeless to me as if they were old photographs I'd pulled from a box in the bottom of my mind.

I gave up on my right brain and switched to a more logical mode. "Janice's father mentioned that she took this route home from law school three times a week. That's a fairly predictable schedule, so I suppose it would be easy enough to time her arrival at this spot."

McGowan had that spellbound look again as he stared down at Del Dios. "You're exactly right," he said.

"But let me play devil's advocate," I went on. "If someone

had rolled Huerte down this driveway, wouldn't the difference in the speed and direction of Huerte's car have been evident from skid marks and body damage? Wouldn't that stuff have come out during your department's investigation of the accident?"

"Had an investigation been vigorously pursued, sure. But I told you, nobody in the department wanted to play. We're talking drunk driving here. The department has enough to do, et cetera, et cetera."

Once again, so many, many things the unsuspecting public doesn't know.

"Elizabeth," McGowan said, "do you, um, sense anything here?"

"Like what?"

"I don't know. Bad vibes." I didn't respond immediately, and after a pause he added, "Because I sure do."

I tried to tune in but picked up nothing but static. "You know, I honestly can't tell. I've been bombarded by bad vibes all day long."

"You seem a little—" I could practically hear him searching for a tactful word.

I finished his sentence for him. "I'm hungry and cranky."

"Well let's grab something to eat, then."

"I'm not exactly dressed."

"I've got a sweatshirt in the car, and the place I'm thinking of, what you're wearing won't matter."

Just a few hundred yards from where we'd parked, McGowan turned off Del Dios Drive. A steep winding road led down the mountainside to a restaurant near the bottom of the valley. There was a nice view of the lake from the parking lot. Inside, a sign near the entrance invited us to take a seat. A pair of red menus were already sitting on the table.

"*Catfish? Rabbit?* What is this, the Road Kill Café?" My

nose was buried in the menu so I didn't hear the waitress come up behind us. McGowan cleared his throat and kicked me under the table.

"You know what you want here?" Our waitress wore pretty teal culottes and matching leather sandals. She was being polite about it, pretending she hadn't heard me.

"I'll have the catfish," McGowan said, handing over his menu. "It's excellent, Elizabeth, really."

"I'm sure you're right, but I'm afraid I can't eat cat anything," I answered. The waitress smiled. My eyes raced around the menu, searching for anything vegetarian. "Ah—I'll take the baked potato and a side of coleslaw. And coffee with cream."

McGowan gathered up the menus and handed them back to our waitress. "Coffee for me, too," he said, stifling a yawn.

When she walked away, he spoke. "So," he said, regarding me kindly with his enormous brown eyes. Looking into them, I felt a lot less cranky.

"What am I to think, McGowan?" I said. "Lunch yesterday, dessert last night, now we're having dinner together—"

"We have to stop eating like this," he said.

I laughed. The cranky curse was completely broken. "You look handsome as always, but tired," I said.

He smiled sleepily. "Never did get that nap."

"You poor thing. Let me bring you up to date quickly, then. I saw an aura yesterday."

"That's nice, dear." He was using that tone people usually reserve for the very slow, the very misguided, or the outright insane. I ignored him.

"No, it wasn't nice. It was red, and angry, and disturbing. It belonged to Janice's boss, an insufferable lout."

"What did Janice do, careerwise?"

"She worked for a real estate investment firm. Here"—I reached for my purse and began digging—"I've got some brochures in here somewhere that should give you an idea." I worked at it several minutes but the excavation was unsuccessful. "That's funny. I could have sworn I put those things back into the book I was reading—"

"What are you reading?" he asked.

"Rereading," I elaborated. "Tom Robbins." I flopped my paperback copy of *Jitterbug Perfume* onto the table and resumed my search. The brochures were nowhere to be found. "Damn it, I must have left them on the beach."

"I love Robbins. Especially *Another Roadside Attraction*." McGowan picked up the book with one hand and covered his yawning mouth with the other.

"How could I have done that?"

"Done what?"

"I hate losing things. I'm always afraid my mind's going to be next."

I was surprised when McGowan didn't make the cheap shot about my mind already being lost. Instead he asked, "So does a red aura mean Janice's boss killed her?"

I was still digging for the brochures and getting a bit annoyed. "I don't know. There's a lot of legwork yet to do. I suppose it's a possibility, but at this point I have no idea what his motive might have been."

"I think we ought to pursue the boyfriend. Janice had a restraining order against the guy. It's the most logical hypothesis."

"I already told you," I said, giving up and putting down my purse. "Alan Katz is not a suspect. Don't waste your mental energy on that."

McGowan shrugged and took a swig of ice water. "I know," he said, "maybe the illegal alien, Huerte, was the intended victim. Maybe Janice was just in the wrong place at the wrong time."

We stared at each other, thinking. The waitress brought our coffee and we both smiled up at her.

"Maybe they were *both* intended victims," I said. The waitress appeared not to listen as she placed our mugs on the table, but I sensed her intense interest. "Did you hear anything about the accident near here last Friday?" I asked her.

She placed a small saucer of creams between McGowan and me, then swiped at the table with a dishcloth. "I saw it," she stated.

"Really," I said. McGowan and I exchanged a surprised glance.

She sighed deeply and nodded her head. "I was just getting off my shift. Ten o'clock. I was driving up toward Del Dios—you can see the road from down here. That car just came flyin' over the edge." She closed her eyes and shuddered. "I'll never forget that sight as long as I live."

"Just one car?" I asked.

"Then the other one, after. But it didn't fly the way that first car did. It sounds funny, but I thought that first car was an airplane 'cause all I could really see was these headlights flyin' through the dark."

"Did you talk to the police?" McGowan asked.

"No. I drove up there, but there was already a couple a cars stopped and people flagging traffic by. So, you know, I figured somebody'd called the police and all."

"You didn't actually see the impact, then," I said.

"No, like I said, I just saw that first car come flyin'—"

"And then the other one," McGowan said.

"Yeah."

McGowan fished in his wallet and handed her a card. "Give me a call if you remember anything else."

She took the card and nodded. She turned and glanced back at the kitchen. "Hey, I think your order's up," she said, stepping away.

"Her description fits our hypothesis exactly," McGowan said, wide-eyed. "What a weird coincidence."

"No such thing."

"No such thing as what?"

"No such thing as a coincidence. The universe is perfectly ordered. No coincidences. We were meant to run into her here."

McGowan looked at me as if he were reconsidering the possibility that I was a borderline flake. Maybe I'd even crossed over that line. "So what color is my aura?" he asked.

"I haven't the foggiest idea."

"Why not?"

"Because," I said, sipping my coffee, "I can't see it."

"Why not?"

I shook my head and laughed. "I already told you. These are not circus tricks. I'm not one of those palm readers with the neon hands flashing over their doorways. Periodically, I have flashes of what is known as 'psychic' insight. But primarily I'm an investigator. My occasional psychic ability is just one of my leveraging tools. Like that gun in your holster. Nice when I can use it, but I can't always count on it."

"So you can't see my aura?" I could tell he was genuinely disappointed.

"Sorry."

Our waitress approached with our meal. She slid the plates onto the table and said, "I wish I could tell you guys more, but it was so dark that night all I really could see was headlights. Both drivers died, didn't they? I heard it on the news. That road"—she shook her head and glanced sideways at me—"that road is scary."

"Hey, thanks for talking to us," I said. "Do you mind if I ask your name?"

"Stacy," she smiled. "Stacy Sanders. I've worked here nine years. Don't worry, I'm not going anywhere. And if I can think of anything else, I'll sure call ya."

After dinner McGowan dropped me off at my car and I wished him sweet dreams. He definitely looked like he could use forty winks. When I arrived home I found three messages on my machine. My mom had called to say she was looking into Pacific Properties's history and financial statements and would get back to me as soon as possible. Janice

Freeman's father, Paul, had called and left a number. And Alan Katz had returned my call. I rewound the tape and listened to the message a second time.

"Hi, Elizabeth. Alan Katz. Sorry I missed you. Actually, I was going to call you. I really would like to talk. I think I'm up to it. It's five-thirty now. I'll be hoping to see you at that Denny's again at eight tonight. Don't bother to call me back because I won't be here. Hope I see you there."

It was already eight o'clock, which is why I ran out of the house in such a rush. That was probably what saved my life.

22

Here's how it all came down: I figured I just might catch up with Katz if I hustled fast enough. I threw on a pair of jeans and flew down the stairs two at a time. The drive to Denny's took about twenty minutes so I'd have to speed, but Katz tended to run late himself, I'd noticed. I grabbed my car keys and as I was running out the door, realized I'd forgotten my purse.

It all seemed to happen at once. I bounded onto the brick walk, remembered my purse, skidded to a stop on the balls of my feet. As I was spinning around I caught a flash near the street out of the corner of my eye. There was a loud crack like unexpected thunder and I heard a distinct pop as the bullet entered the wall just inches from my head.

In dreams I'm often paralyzed by fear. My legs won't obey my command to run, or they feel as if I'm thigh-deep in mud. Tonight, though, my legs were in motion before my brain even engaged. I think I realized what was happening about the time I was careering down the hall to the bedrooms. Cold fear rose through me and I could feel my heart banging against the inside of my chest. Its muffled beat throbbed so loudly in my ears I couldn't hear a thing. The sudden deafness panicked me even more. What if footsteps were gaining on me and I couldn't even hear them? As I reached the edge of hysteria a voice inside my mind said,

Everything's going to be all right. In the next moment I knew my game plan.

My old house has a back bedroom equipped with a midget-sized door. The little door opens onto a path between the hedge and the back of the house; the path leads to a hole in the fence along the street. In the old days I suppose this funny little door had served as a discreet passage to the outhouse. I'm sure no one in history ever made a more urgent exit through it than I did that night.

The hedge provided cover all the way to the street, and I was able to collect my wits a bit as I scurried through the foliage. Once I hit the open sidewalk, though, I felt alarmingly vulnerable. I willed my fear into the muscles of my legs and pounded past the houses and trees of my neighborhood. I knew many of my neighbors well but didn't dare risk drawing danger to them by stopping for assistance.

A half mile down Juniper I ran into The Minstrel, a coffee house/music bar catering to latter-day bohemians. The owner, my buddy Mel, caught one look at my beet red face and huffing body bounding through the door and quickly motioned me into the kitchen with a concerned expression. He fixed a glass of water and said, "Should I call the police?"

I leaned over, hands on my knees and head down. I nodded as I gulped deep, slow breaths. He dialed 911 and when the call went through, handed the phone to me.

"Shots are being fired at three one three two Juniper in Escondido. Yes, three one three two!" I panted. "Hurry!" I disconnected and caught the question mark on Mel's face. "If you tell them too much, especially things like, 'No, no one's been hurt,' they won't get there for hours," I explained. I took a draw from the water glass and then dialed McGowan's pager, punching in the number on Mel's phone after the beeps. McGowan called back in a matter of seconds.

"Tom, it's Elizabeth. Someone took a shot at me about five minutes ago outside my house. I'm at The Minstrel coffee house down the street. The cops have already been called to my place. Pick me up here."

"Were you hit?"

"No."

"I'm on my way."

The scene around my house looked like a cop carnival. Several blue-and-whites were parked at odd angles in the driveway and along the street, their flashing lights illuminating the yard with an eerie amber glow. Uniformed and plainclothes police swarmed in and out among the cars, along the bushes, and up and down the front walk. Tom pulled into the driveway and parked the car. He reached over to the passenger's side and took me by the arm.

"You okay?" he asked.

"Honestly? It's hard to tell. I'm not quite all here. I feel like I'm having the kind of dream you have when you eat too many chilies before bed. Know what I mean?"

He smiled and squeezed my arm.

"Has anyone ever shot at you, Tom?"

He nodded. So he was an old hand at this stuff.

I shook my head in wonderment. "Great job, law enforcement. Occupational hazards, yes, but so exciting. Of course, if you really think about it, with an office job you stand a good chance of being stabbed in the back. This business of being out-and-out shot at is comparatively refreshing."

A uniformed officer had emerged from one of the police cars and was walking toward our car.

"That's my partner, Rodney," Tom said. "Come on. He's expecting us."

Rodney, a stocky man in his forties with a ruddy complexion and graying red hair, was somber and polite. "You must be Elizabeth. Rodney Chessman," he said, nodding curtly. He raised his pale, bushy eyebrows and held up a clipboard. "Ready for this?"

"Sure."

"Let's have a look, then."

Rodney motioned to the other officers and they followed me along the brick walkway to the front porch, where I pointed out a half-inch hole in the outside wall. "The shot came from the street—the bullet entered here," I said.

McGowan walked over and cautiously opened the front door. The rest of us followed him into the house. We walked along the inside wall of the living room, to the place where the bullet had come through. Large pieces of plaster lay on the floor, leaving a hole in the wall at least six inches wide. McGowan squatted from his great height onto his heels and peered through the gap. "And this is where the bullet exited," he stated, surveying the damage. He got up and I followed him across the room to a smaller cavity in the wall, where something messy and metallic was embedded in the plaster. "And where it stopped," he said with finality.

I thought back to the flash I'd seen near the street, quickly calculating the distance this little bullet had traveled. "Holy shit," I said.

"Excuse me," Rodney called to me. "Were these here before you left the house?"

We looked up to see Rodney pointing to the middle of the room, where a distinct trail of footprints muddied the carpet from the tile entryway, across the carpeted living room, and down the hall. The muddy prints stopped at the stairs.

I stared dumbly at the footprints, trying to comprehend their implication: that someone had come in uninvited, that someone had tracked mud onto my floor with no regard whatever for the new carpet, that someone carrying a gun had pursued me into my own home. . . .

Suddenly my stomach seemed to be falling through my abdomen, heading for the floor. "Whitman!" I cried out, sailing up two stairs at a time. I could hear Tom and Rodney coming up after me, calling out for me to wait.

"Whitman? Baby?" I rushed into my upstairs bedroom, afraid of what I might see. "Whitman! Whitman!" My voice was hoarse with desperation. A little meow issued from under the bed before I got too carried away. "Oh, thank God."

Tom and Rodney walked in to find me practically smothering the little cat with kisses. When I looked up I felt the tears streaming down my face. I hadn't even realized I'd been crying. Tom knelt down beside me on the floor and put his arm around my shoulders. "It's okay now," he said softly.

Suddenly I felt ridiculous. Cats know how to fend for themselves; I knew that. For a brief moment I was able to detach from my feelings a bit and recognize in myself the beginnings of post-traumatic stress syndrome. That's a fancy psychological term for the living hell people often suffer after being confronted suddenly and imminently with death. Victims of violent crime exhibit a cluster of symptoms—jumpiness, an all-pervasive fear, shame, humiliation. I'd seen it in some of my women clients, victims of rape and abuse who turned the outrage of these violations onto themselves, questioning what *they* did to cause the event, rather than directing the anger outward.

"Excuse me," I said, jumping to my feet. I walked to the side of the bed and looked over at Tom and Rodney, who appeared perplexed. "This will take only a few minutes, don't be alarmed. I'm just going to do a little processing here."

They looked at each other and shrugged.

I pulled the pillows into a neat little pile and took a deep breath. Slowly I raised my fists into the air and came down on the bedding with everything I had.

"GODDAMN - MOTHER - FUCKING - SON - OF - A - FUCKING-BITCH!" I screamed in a deep, rhythmic voice, punctuating each word with a resounding pummeling of the pillows. I really let it roar. I think I'd gone about three rounds when the puzzled faces of the other officers appeared in the doorway. I heard Tom say, "It's okay, she's a psychologist, she knows what she's doing."

Inhaling deeply, I felt a powerful calm surging through my body and mind. I turned to the baffled group at the door and smiled. "Better!" I assured them.

Rodney, Tom, and I sat at the kitchen table, filling out the report. "Approximately what time did the shooting occur?" Rodney asked.

At the mention of time I suddenly remembered my date with Alan. "Oh, my God, I was supposed to meet Alan at eight." I glanced at my watch: 8:43. "Excuse me, I have to make a phone call," I said.

"Whoa, whoa, whoa! Just a minute there." Tom grabbed my arm as I jumped up from my chair. "When did you make plans to see Alan?"

"I didn't, really. He left a message on my machine while you and I were at dinner. He told me he'd meet me again, same time, same place."

"So Alan knew you'd be leaving the house tonight." Tom stared at me like an impatient schoolteacher, as if the correct conclusion were painfully obvious.

"He knew I might be, yes."

"Where were you going to meet him?"

"The Denny's on Black Mountain Road."

Tom picked up his two-way and radioed some cryptic message that I took to be a call to someone in the field to head over to Denny's.

"What's he look like?" he asked me.

I gave him a brief description, which Tom repeated onto the airwaves. I knew he was chasing down the wrong trail. I also knew he was just doing his job.

The two-way continued to burp and spurt noisily as we finished up the report. After one such eruption Tom grabbed the device and spoke intently into it. When he was done he turned to me and said, "They picked Alan up at the restaurant. We'll talk to him downtown."

Oh, boy, Alan's gonna love me for this, I thought.

23

The nearly empty parking lot and cut-back staff gave the Escondido police station an eerie after-hours feel. If you've ever entered the deserted aisles of a twenty-four-hour grocery store late at night, you know the hollow ambiance I'm talking about. I followed McGowan past the reception area and into a room about ten feet square. It was as sparse as a room could be without being completely empty: bare white windowless walls, a card table, two folding chairs. Sitting up straight in one of the chairs, hands crossed placidly on the table before him, was Alan Katz. His red curls glowed brightly under the harsh light of the fluorescent panel overhead. He looked up with luminous blue eyes as we entered, and the briefest of smiles crossed his lips when he saw me.

McGowan, towering over Alan, placed his hands on his hips and said, "Okay, Mr. Katz, I understand you've already talked to Sergeant Lewis. If you don't mind, Dr. Chase here has a few more questions."

Alan nodded. "Sure, no problem."

McGowan pulled the other chair out for me to sit, handed me the paperwork Sergeant Lewis had been filling out, then leaned over and spoke into my ear. "I'll be in my office—upstairs, third cubicle on the left—when you're done here." He gave Alan a good hard stare, then left the tiny room, shutting the door behind him.

"You're a doctor?" Alan's expression was friendly, quizzical.

"I used to practice psychotherapy."

"Huh. From psychotherapy to criminal investigation—that's a weird career path."

"Yes, I suppose it is."

We stared across the table at each other for a few moments without speaking. I was the one to finally break the silence. "What are you doing for a living these days, Alan?"

"Back to my old job—construction. Humbling, but it pays the bills."

"Constructing what?"

"You know the new California Center for the Arts here in town?"

What Escondidan didn't know of the new arts center? Our little podunk city had shocked greater metropolitan San Diego by appropriating a few million in the name of culture. The center itself was to be an immense and stunning structure. Like many worthwhile government endeavors, it would require a significant chunk of the budget. I was among the small group of taxpayers who applauded the construction and paid no heed to the naysayers. Slave labor aside, there were undoubtedly plenty of Egyptians who had grumbled about the high price of those damn pyramids, too.

"You're working on the arts center?" I asked with interest.

"Yeah. I'm enjoying it, too." Alan smiled, gracing the room with his dimples. "Incredible architecture. Work I can actually take pride in."

I glanced at the sheet McGowan had handed me. It gave Alan's particulars—name, height, weight, serial number. "This says you're living in Escondido," I said. "I thought you lived out on Silver Branch Road in Ramona."

He looked puzzled. "How'd you know I used to live there?"

"That was the address listed on the restraining order Janice had served on you, not too long before her death."

"Oh. Actually I haven't lived in Ramona for years. Long story. My ex and our daughter live out there. When Janice broke up with me I wanted to make her jealous, so I told her I was moving back in with Tanya. I guess she believed me. Don't think it made her jealous, though."

"So you weren't living in Ramona when the restraining order was served?"

"No. I've been in Escondido the whole time. The marshal who served the thing on me finally tracked me down at work."

He was talking easily, the way people do when they're telling the truth.

"You look better, Alan."

He did. The desperation was gone. His relaxed body language communicated an acceptance of self, an acceptance of me, an acceptance of the moment. The self-conscious charm had, for the time being, been turned off, which made him all the more charming.

"I feel like shit," he answered flatly. "Life is just really stark and hard right now."

"Death is pretty stark, isn't it?"

He looked down at the tabletop and shook his head. "I wanted to get high so bad last night. You know, I struggled with it for about an hour in my car after you left. In fact—"

He looked up at me, excitement rising in his voice.

"—I was driving out of the parking lot to go get fucked up when a guy from my NA meeting drove in. When he rolled down his window to say hi he took one look at my face and said, 'Get in the car, man.' He hung out with me all night, talking it out. I think about that now and it blows my mind. I mean, what are the chances that was a coincidence?"

Humility had definitely enhanced Alan's appeal. "You're asking the wrong person," I answered. "I'm not a big believer in coincidences."

He nodded. "Really. So, can you tell me what's going on here?"

I decided it would be time-effective to get straight to the point. "Someone tried to shoot me tonight. The police thought it might be you. That's what's going on here."

Alan clamped his long fingers over his mouth. His bright blue eyes widened, the black pupils dilating like spreading ink. "Jesus," was all he managed to say.

"Sergeant Lewis didn't clue you in?"

"So that's what this is all about," he said, a light going on in his mind. "No, nobody told me anything. The cops just kept asking me where I'd been the last two hours. I kept telling them that if they didn't believe me they should go talk to the guy who'd been pouring my coffee at Denny's the last hour and a half—remember the geeky kid with the radical skater cut?"

I thought of our chalk-faced young waiter from last night and nodded. Who could forget?

"Same guy. They finally talked to him and the manager, and I guess several customers saw me there, too. Accounted for my whereabouts and all that."

"Well, that's good. So what was it you wanted to meet me about, Alan?"

"Oh, wow. Someone just tried to shoot you and now you're perfectly calm and concerned about what I wanted to meet you about. Pretty impressive."

I laughed. " 'Concerned' is the key word there, Alan. Someone killed Janice and now they're trying to kill me. I'm hoping you'll help me brainstorm."

"Well that's just it, that's what I was going to tell you tonight. I've been thinking about it and I really don't think anyone could have killed Janice. She didn't run in those kind of circles, man. She was—"

He lifted a hand into the air, as if he were hoping to snatch the right word. "She was . . ."

He wasn't having much luck.

"Perhaps someone hated her for being so good," I suggested.

He combed the curly red hair above his brow with his attenuated fingers, then rested his forehead on his hand. "No, it must have been an accident."

"Alan, someone tried to shoot me tonight."

"Maybe that was unrelated—"

"Come on, I already told you where I stand on coincidences. Think. What about Pacific Properties? Did anyone at work have anything against her?"

"She wasn't a threat to anybody, if that's what you mean. She was great at her job, but her sights were set elsewhere. Janice really didn't give a damn about Pacific Properties, to tell you the truth."

"What about Stan Ellis?"

"Janice's boss? He thought the world of her, man. He wouldn't fart without consulting her first."

"Perhaps Janice knew too much. Did she ever mention anything to you about fraudulent reporting of the company's assets?"

He paused for a second, index finger in the air. "Wait a minute. Yeah. Um, well, first you need to get the picture. I wasn't so much on the administrative end, like she was. I was out in the field mostly, checking on the company's properties and stuff. I didn't really pay much attention to anything except Janice back then, which is part of why I lost my job. But anyway, now that you mention it, there was some stink about Pacific Properties taking big fees and some investors being pissed off or something."

"What was Janice's role in all this?"

"Role? I don't exactly know. But she seemed to find it amusing more than anything. You gotta understand, her ultimate goal was to be a superior court judge. She was going to law school, you know. Studying law was her life. All the little soap operas at work didn't interest her much."

He sighed heavily and hung his head. "The little soap operas with me probably didn't either."

He glanced at me just briefly, but the pain and regret in that look pierced my heart. I regarded the beautiful man sitting across the table and thought back to what Janice's journal had to say about her split with Alan, the part about how a bad break takes a long time to heal. I was about to comment when he went on in a shaky voice.

"What's killing me is that now I can't . . . say I'm sorry."

Tears had crowded into the corners of his eyes and he swiped at them before they had a chance to spill over. He laughed nervously. "Everybody keeps telling me that when you stop numbing out with drugs you start to feel your feelings. They're not kidding." He rolled his eyes with embarrassment. "It's a good thing you're a shrink—every time I see you I start crying."

"I think it's pretty normal under the circumstances," I said.

The tiny room was silent.

"You know, Alan," I said after a time, "I think if you tell Janice you're sorry, she'll still hear you."

He hissed scornfully. "People believe that life-after-death stuff because it makes them feel better. The opiate of the masses and all."

"Well, in my case it's based on scientific opinion. I happen to be a trained parapsychologist—that's where the 'doctor' in Doctor Chase comes from. I've seen study upon study upon study, and I can tell you that the current evidence pointing to life after death is weighty. I say odds are Janice will hear you."

"Odds? I thought you didn't believe in coincidences."

"Just talk to her, Alan," I said softly.

"Okay. Maybe I will." He crossed his arms over his chest and hugged himself unconsciously.

I pushed back my chair and was about to suggest we hit

the road when an idea crossed my mind. "Can you wait here just a couple more minutes, please?"

He was off in a private world and looked at me absent mindedly. "Sure, no problem."

"I'll be right back."

I rushed up the darkened stairwell. It opened onto a large floor, also nearly dark. A single panel of fluorescent lighting illuminated a cubicle on the left of the room. I walked toward the light and found McGowan sitting at his desk, leafing through a *Guns and Ammo* magazine. "All done?" he said, looking up.

"Would you happen to have a picture of Michael Huerte in the file by now?"

"Let me look."

He got up, stifling another yawn, and pulled a manila folder from a metal file cabinet beside his desk. He flipped through the contents of the file. "Bingo." He handed the photo across the desk to me.

It was a head shot. Huerte's dead eyes stared blankly. Even for a black-and-white photo, the guy looked awfully gray. "Ew," I couldn't help but say. "Thanks."

I started back down the darkened stairs. The photo in my hand sent a chill to the center of my gut. I thought back to my own stairs at home, where the muddy footprints on my carpet had stopped. I paused on the landing, then turned and walked back upstairs to McGowan's cubicle. He looked up and smiled sleepily.

"Can I spend the night at your house?" I asked.

He made an "O" with his mouth. "You brazen hussy."

"More like cowardly scaredy-cat," I replied honestly.

"More like smart girl," McGowan said. "Sure. I'd feel a lot better if you did."

I started back downstairs.

"But Elizabeth," he called out.

"Yeah?" I yelled over my shoulder.

"You risk being hit on, either way."

"Promises, promises," I called back.

"Never seen him in my life," Alan said, holding the mug shot of Michael Huerte and shaking his head. "He doesn't take a very good picture, does he?"

"Oh, I don't know. Considering he's dead I think he looks pretty good."

"What?"

"This is the man who was driving the car that ran into Janice's. He was also pronounced dead at the scene. Look again. Do you have any idea who this is?"

Alan gazed down at the photo in his hands. He didn't say a word.

"Alan?"

He nodded his head. "Yeah, that's it all right."

"It? Who?"

"Stark. Like you said, death is stark." He handed the photo back.

"You don't know him."

"No, I don't. Sorry."

24

"I need to stop home first."

McGowan had just turned off the freeway and we were now heading east on Ninth Avenue. It was fascinating, riding in a police car. Suddenly the freeways and roads were filled with the most courteous drivers you ever did see. I personally had never seen four lanes of traffic maintain a perfect fifty-five miles per hour. It was a power rush at first, watching reckless citizens very much like myself shaping up at the mere threat of a traffic ticket. But the novelty wore off and the pace got annoying pretty quickly.

McGowan didn't take his eyes off the road.

"People don't usually drive like this, you know," I said.

"I know. When I'm not in the cruiser I get to see the anarchy that truly reigns on our freeways." He smiled. "What's even better is, I get to participate in it."

"Thanks again, Tom," I said.

"For what?"

"For not leaving me for target practice at my house."

"It's big of me, I know," he said. "In all seriousness, Elizabeth, you're handling this really well. You seem so calm."

"It's that Gestalt therapy I did. Works every time."

"That business of screaming obscenities and pounding pillows? Really?"

"Yeah."

"Do you do that kind of thing often?"

"Only when prodded or provoked." Before he could take that and run with it I quickly added, "Of course, I'm also heartened by the progress we're making on the case. I must be getting close if I'm worth shooting at."

McGowan slowed and turned south on Juniper. He made a loud yawning noise. "Excuse me," he said.

"Long day, huh?"

"Um-hm. But I've had longer. What'd you find out from the boyfriend—anything?"

"Nothing. That's one of the reasons I have to stop at home. I've gone as far as I can go without assistance. I need to consult a cosmic map."

"A cosmic map."

"Yes. You'll see."

McGowan pulled into my driveway. The cop carnival had packed up and traveled on. In the bleak illumination of a lone porch light, the bullet hole in the side of the house wasn't even visible. This was my own home, but to me it felt strangely empty, more like a movie theater after the crowds have departed.

"Hey, Tom," I said, unbuckling my seat belt, "cover me to the front door, will you?"

Our trip to the front door was uneventful, but I wasn't prepared for what I saw inside. In addition to the muddy footprints, clouds of purple-black fingerprint dust darkened tabletops and whole patches of the floor and walls. The house looked as physically abused as any battered wife, and my heart went out to her. Whitman ran to my ankles, and between rubbings loudly apprised me of the disruptions to his usually orderly life.

"Do you think we're safe in here?" I asked.

McGowan pulled a revolver from his police belt. He twirled it in his hand, Quick Draw McGraw style, then aimed at the window in one smooth motion. It all came off as a pretty slick trick. "Yeah," he said, "I think we'll live."

I tsked and shook my head disdainfully, pretending I

wasn't impressed by his antics. Liar that I was.

"Of course I, personally, am in danger of starving to death," he added. "Have you got any food around here?"

"Help yourself to anything in the fridge," I said. "I'm going to make a couple of phone calls from my office here before it gets too late, if it isn't already."

I had just dialed the number Janice's father had left on my machine earlier that day when McGowan yelled, "Hey, I meant people food! I see stuff for rabbits and horses in here, but—"

The phone on the other end of the line started to ring. "Quiet! I'm on the phone!" I laughed.

I said "shit" under my breath when I got a recording for the corporate offices of the very famous restaurant company that Paul Freeman was president of, although I was half expecting that anyway.

"I might be starving but I refuse to eat alfalfa sprouts," McGowan grumbled loudly.

"There are some frozen burritos in the freezer," I called back. "I assume you know how to operate a microwave." Next I dialed my mom.

"Hello?"

"Hey, Mom. Sorry to call late. I was wondering if you'd had a chance to—"

"Nothing to be sorry about and yes, I found what you might be looking for on Pacific Properties. Looks like some limited partners filed a lawsuit against the general partner last March—"

McGowan's voice came booming from the kitchen: "Ho! Ice cream! Why didn't you say so!"

"Who's that, dear?"

"Just a friend."

There was a brief pause during which I could hear the wheels in Mom's matchmaker machine turning. Then she went on, "Well, I've got the information on disk and can download it onto your computer if you want—"

"Thanks, Mom. You're great. But can you just print it out and fax it? I'll be running another program on my computer tonight."

"Sure, hon. Hey listen, your dad's home. You want to talk to him?"

"Of course."

I heard some shuffling as the phone changed hands, then my dad's mellow voice came on the line. "Well, hello, honey."

"Hey, Dad. Welcome back to California. What's up?"

"Not a whole heck of a lot. I have something to amuse you with, though."

"Oh, good. I could use some amusement."

"I had a real strange dream about you when I was dozing on the plane home last night."

Dad holds his opinions of all things metaphysical in abeyance. He's waiting for the "conclusive" evidence to come in. That doesn't stop him from having an occasional precognitive dream now and then.

"It was a good dream, I hope."

"It wasn't good or bad, just strange.

"You were wearing my lab coat and working in my laboratory. I could see the Bunsen burner and the chart of the elements in the background quite clearly. You were very intent upon your task, don't ask me what it was. I remember feeling proud—I knew you were on the verge of discovering something very important. But there was danger, too, as if you might be playing with powerful forces, nuclear energy or something."

"Still hoping I'll become a rocket scientist, aren't you, Dad?"

"That interpretation didn't even occur to me. I thought the dream might have some bearing on the case you're working on. But—you're not considering a career change, are you?"

Till the day he dies, my father will probably hold out

hope that I will one day practice medicine. As it is, my work occasionally affords me the opportunity to save lives. That's close enough for me.

"Nope. Still dabbling in psychic detection."

"Is everything all right, Elizabeth?"

"Yeah. Everything's fine." Not a lie, really. At the moment all was kosher.

"God, this is HEAVEN!"

In the throes of orgiastic ice-cream ecstasy, McGowan was getting verbal. Dad, ever tactful, said, "Listen, kid, I don't want to keep you. Take care of yourself, sweetheart. Talk to you soon."

Mom's fax started to come in just as I hung up the phone.

"You've got two Ben & Jerry's and two Haägen-Dasz in there," McGowan proclaimed as he came through the office door. He was eating straight out of the Cherry Garcia carton.

"Okay, all right. So I have this weakness." I had taken a seat at the computer and was busy searching Janice Freeman's file for her birth certificate. I punched in her birth date (09-27-1965), birth time (6:45 PM) and birthplace (San Diego, California, Long. 117W10, Lat. 32N45), adjusted for daylight saving's, and waited.

"Whatcha doin' now?" McGowan walked over and stood behind me. I sensed him back there, looking over my shoulder at the computer screen. I felt my body coming to attention: raised heart rate, increased temperature, the whole deal.

"I'm doing a cosmic map."

"What in the heck is a—"

At that moment the screen brought up a multicolored wheel, which I studied with interest.

"What the hell is that?" McGowan asked.

"What does it look like?"

"I dunno, like a pie chart with Greek letters on it. I give up. What is it?"

"That's Janice Freeman's natal horoscope. Those little marks are called glyphs. Each one represents a planet. You're essentially looking at a map of the sky at the time and place of Janice Freeman's birth."

"Oh, no." He spun my chair around so he could look directly into my eyes. "Come on, Elizabeth, *astrology*? That's a bunch of shit."

I gave him a smile, batted my eyelashes, and spun my chair back so that I could view the screen again. "The stuff you read in the daily paper, yes. That is a bunch of shit. But the real discipline of astrology has been around for more than ten thousand years. There's a lot more to it than dividing the whole world into twelve sun signs and filling column space with hokey advice and vague predictions for each group."

"Like what?"

"Okay. Let's get beyond Janice's sun in Libra, which, by the way, reveals that her life was a quest for balance and justice. From these other planets I can tell you that she was exceptionally intelligent, a hard worker, came from a respectable family, was deeply compassionate and emotionally intense." For each characteristic I pointed out the corresponding planet, bouncing my finger around the chart wheel.

"You can tell all that, really?"

"And a lot more besides."

McGowan sounded troubled. "Like what, predicting the future and all? I mean, even if you could do it, don't you find that depressing and frightening, that life is all predestined? I prefer to stay away from the whole thing."

"Once again, I applaud your skepticism." I leaned back in my chair. "There are a hell of a lot of charlatans out there claiming to practice astrology. If someone tells you such-and-such is absolutely going to happen, watch out."

"But if you can't predict the future, what's the point?"

"The point is guidance. See, a chart is really just a map of what's possible. The planets and signs pinpoint directions, but you're always in the driver's seat. The map can't take you anywhere you don't already want to go."

I printed out Janice's natal chart and created another one for the day of her death.

"Now what's that?" he asked.

"This shows me where the planets were at the time Janice died. When I superimpose these planets onto her natal planets, it tells me what was going on in Janice's life that day." I printed out the chart of the transiting planets and turned off the computer. "Come on. I'm going to go finish this in the kitchen. I want some of that vanilla Swiss almond before we go to your place."

In the kitchen I grabbed the remains of a pint of ice cream and sat at the table to study the new chart. Janice's planets were printed in black; I penned in the position of the planets on the day of her death in red. What they laid bare had my mind spinning.

"So what do you see now? What are all those little black and red things up in the corner of the chart there?"

"Okay," I said, pointing to a cluster of planets on the chart, "these planets are all in Scorpio, Janice's eighth house. The eighth house sometimes represents death, and taxes too, if you can believe that. Right in the middle of the cluster we find Neptune, the mystery planet. Placed here in the eighth house it indicates death under mysterious circumstances. Tell us something we don't know, right?"

McGowan laughed. "You got that right."

He seemed to be following, so I went on. "Anyway, this is Mars, the planet named for the god of war and often associated with destructive energy. As you can see, on the day of Janice's death it was being approached by Pluto here, the planet named for the god of the underworld and also associated with death. That's what they call a conjunction, when two planets align like that."

"It looks like a Pac Man game."

"Yeah, you can look at it that way. Anyway, I was expecting the Mars/Pluto connection. You see it frequently in charts of accidents and crimes. What I wasn't expecting was this."

I pointed to another planet in the cluster, a circle on a cross. The universal symbol of femininity, it represented Venus.

"What's that mean?"

"It could mean a number of things."

"Such as?"

"Venus is associated with several areas in life, typically money or property and material possessions—"

"Well, that narrows it down," McGowan interjected sarcastically.

"But I'll tell you what I think it means here in Janice's chart."

"Okay, what do you think it means?"

I crunched on a chocolate-covered almond and looked up at McGowan. "There's a woman involved in Janice's death."

25

I packed a couple of changes of clothes—baggy brown pants and a tan shirt for daytime, black jeans and a matching T-shirt and turtleneck for night. The idea was to dress as inconspicuously as possible. I had a lot of visits to make in the next day or two and I didn't want to be an easy target. I laughed grimly to myself, thinking how tough it must have been for the unknown marksman to keep an eye on me in my glowing blue bathing suit today.

I gathered up the astrological charts, Mom's fax, and the picture of Michael Huerte that I'd temporarily cadged from the EPD and stuffed the items into my briefcase. I also packed the police file on Janice Freeman and, for good measure, her yellow journal. Everything else, of course, fit into my purse.

I considered bringing Whitman along, but McGowan's neck of the woods was home to a significant coyote population. I decided my cat would fare better at home. I filled his water bowl and made certain his self-feeding gizmo was fully stocked with kibble.

"Will I need a sleeping bag?" I asked McGowan.

"I do have a guest room, and I believe there are actually sheets on the bed. Of course, you're always welcome to sleep with . . . Nero, on the couch."

I gave him a ha-ha-very-funny look and said, "I've laid with meaner curs, I'm sure."

We decided to leave my car—a bright red Mustang—in my garage. Enthusiastically cooperating with my low-profile plan, McGowan said he'd be happy to loan me a '68 Dodge Charger he kept in his garage.

"Does it go?" I asked.

"I rebuilt the engine myself," he replied. As if that answered the question.

"Yes, but does it go?"

"It goes," McGowan said, smiling slyly.

The first half of our trip to McGowan's we rode in silence. I kept a vigilant watch for tails in the rearview mirror, but once we hit the rural back roads it was clear that no one was behind us, not for at least a mile, anyway.

McGowan observed my rubbernecking without comment. Finally he said, "It's getting to you now, isn't it?"

"What? The assassination attempt? Heck, no. It's the IRS I'm worried about." I heard him chuckle under his breath. "Yes, it's getting to me."

"When we get home we'll take care of that," he said. I wondered what he meant but was too chicken to ask. We turned onto a straightaway and picked up speed.

"Ever been married, Elizabeth?"

Now here was a subject that was bound to cheer me.

"Me? Technically, no."

"What do you mean, technically?"

"I spent most of my twenties with a man, but I—ha!—had a bad feeling about it, so I diligently avoided all legal ties. Didn't matter. I didn't escape unscathed. The breakup was just as debilitating as the real McCoy. World fell apart, finances were in a shambles, the whole nine yards. How about you?"

"Basically I'm too strange to get married."

"Yes, but you recognize it, and that's the first step to change." I shot him a just-kidding smile.

He grinned. "Nope, never been married. Came close, though. Such was my luck that three weeks short of the wedding my fiancée joined a religious cult."

"You're kidding."

"About this, I do not kid. She started hanging out with the Church of the Risen Lord. Before I knew it, it was Tom McGowan versus Jesus Christ. Their version of him, anyway."

"Jesus," I said, "that's pretty tough competition."

"Afraid I couldn't compete. Hell, I'm lucky if I manage to bring home a bag of groceries, let alone multiply loaves and fishes."

I tried to keep my giggling politely subdued, because as funny as he was, McGowan looked pained.

"So she seriously just went off the deep end?"

He nodded.

"I'm sorry."

He drove silently for a while, lost in a memory somewhere. Then he looked over at me and smiled. "Women, what good are they, anyway? Always leaving the damn toilet seat up."

"Hey," I countered. "You think that's bad, you should try living with a man sometime. Panty hose draped all over the shower. It's enough to make you sick."

We were laughing as we pulled into McGowan's driveway. Something about Nero bounding through the door to greet us—or perhaps just the knowledge that there was enough firepower in his house to squelch a small insurgence—went a long way toward quelling my remaining fears.

I did my best to pet Nero, although my hands were full with my briefcase and oversized bag. "Here, let me take your things," McGowan said, unloading me. "I'm going to put these in the guest room. Have a seat in here. I'll be right back."

I wandered into the living room and again admired the volumes lining McGowan's shelves.

"So what's with all the books?" I called toward the back of the house.

"I was a high school English teacher in a former life," he called back.

"No kidding?"

"Yeah, but it got too dangerous." McGowan lowered his voice as he walked back into the room. "Gangs, plummeting SAT scores, underage girls coming on to me. I needed less stress in my life. Switched over to police work. Can I get you anything—hot chocolate, maybe?"

"Look," I said, "I know how tired you are—"

"No, listen. I'm fine. After all that ice cream at your place, I'm on a giddy sugar high. You can't leave me alone now. Besides, we need to get you taken care of here." He put his hands on my shoulders and gently pushed me onto the sofa. "Wait here, I'll be right back."

I don't know what, exactly, I'd been expecting, but the worn black leather bag he brought in from the front closet wasn't it.

"Okay," he said taking a seat next to me on the sofa, "this ought to do you nicely."

He pulled out the sleek black Glock forty-five semiautomatic and handed it to me, barrel pointed toward the floor. "You seemed to take to this piece the other night. I want you to carry it on you at all times for the next few days. Don't go leaving it in the car, all right? I have a holster if you need one. Now remember, there's no safety switch— just squeeze hard. The magazine carries—"

"Thirteen rounds, plus one in the chamber. I remember." I popped the magazine out. It was empty. "You think I'll need bullets, too?"

McGowan rummaged in the leather bag and came out with a box of forty-five-caliber hollow points. He reached for the magazine in my hand.

"No," I said, pushing his hand away, "let me do this. You

just relax." I gave his chest a little shove and he fell back onto the sofa. One by one I popped the rounds into the magazine. They were fat, as bullets go, and on the heavy side. I built up a gratifying rhythm, pushing them into the spring-loaded slots.

"You're very good with your hands," he said languidly, watching me through half-closed eyelids.

In truth, loading the gun was a relaxing process. My hands did need something to do. Besides, I never had learned how to knit.

I worked quietly, but my mind was busy sifting and sorting the events of the day. Finally I broke the silence. "I'm going to go pay a visit to the man with the red aura tomorrow. Which reminds me, I need to read that fax Mom sent about Pacific Properties. There's something not right about Janice's boss, Stan Ellis. What I can't figure out is, which woman in Janice's life was I picking up on in her death chart? I'm pretty sure I saw two men, not a woman, in that astral dream. I never told you about my astral travel trip, did I?"

McGowan didn't answer. I glanced over. He was gone to the world, his head lying against the sofa cushion, his chest rising and falling in a slow rhythm. His eyes, large and darkly lashed, were achingly beautiful in sleep. I was tempted to reach over and touch them but didn't dare wake him.

"Come on, Nero," I said to the hound, "let's go to bed."

26

McGowan had already left for work by the time I woke up the next morning. I wandered barefoot through the empty house and found a set of keys he'd left for me on the kitchen table, along with a note. In its own way the note was thoughtful, perhaps even tender: *Don't forget the Glock.*

I showered as if I had all the time in the world, a clear message from my subconscious that I wasn't thrilled about getting on with the day. McGowan's towels were plush, colossal, emerald-colored things that put the severe little wipes I kept in my guest bath to shame. The sheets on his guest bed, too, had been thick and sumptuous, probably one of those mega-thread-count brands I'm too cheap to buy. I wrapped myself in the ample velvety towel and decided that McGowan was probably a better housekeeper than I was.

I padded out into the kitchen, where I found coffee and a refrigerator brimming with too many choices: eggs, bacon, strawberries, muffins, deli roast beef and turkey slices, left-over lasagna, yogurt, cantaloupe. At this point I had to concede McGowan's domestic superiority. I cut a slice of melon, poured a cup of coffee, and sat down at the kitchen table to read the research on Pacific Properties that Mom had faxed me.

She'd found the article in a recent issue of *Financial Planning*: "Trouble in Paradise: Pacific Properties Under Fire." I laughed out loud and cried, "Number seven!" Allow me to explain. I'm keeping a running count of the number of California exposé articles that use the old "trouble in paradise" headline. This was the seventh I'd seen this year. The subhead read: "Western Real Estate Mogul Alexander Spiro Contends with Angry Investors." Apparently the managing general partner of Pacific Properties—not Janice's boss, Stan Ellis, but presumably his boss, Alexander Spiro—was being sued by about two hundred investors who claimed that Spiro had "misappropriated funds." The limited partners asserted that the guy had pocketed over $1.5 million rightfully belonging to them, and a San Diego superior court had ruled in the investors' favor. The case was currently pending appeal.

I put the article aside and poured another cup of coffee. From the phone on the wall I called the number Janice Freeman's father had left on my machine yesterday.

"Mr. Freeman's office. This is Laurel." The voice was friendly, without a trace of corner office stuffiness.

"Hello, Laurel. This is Elizabeth Chase, returning Mr. Freeman's call."

"Oh, yes. Hello there. He told me you might be calling. He's not in today, but he asked me to give you his home phone number. He's eager to speak with you."

She gave me a number with a Rancho Santa Fe prefix and wished me a nice day.

At that point I'd done just about everything I could do without leaving the house. I dressed in my baggy brown clothes and made the guest bed. I picked up the keys McGowan had left on the table and dutifully packed the Glock into my purse. At the last minute I remembered to check the bathrooms. I wanted to be sure to leave the toilet seats up.

I stood in the front hallway and considered borrowing McGowan's bulletproof vest. If he was like most roommates, he'd hate it if I snagged his clothes without asking first. Besides, the vest looked awfully heavy and the day looked awfully hot.

"Hey, Nero, want to go for a ride?"

The hound napping on the floor didn't even lift his head. He merely raised his eyes in a "who, me?" expression.

"Okay, then just walk me to the car."

As I opened the front door I was blasted by a wall of heat. It was going to be another uncharacteristically hot and humid day in San Diego County. Nero didn't budge. I figured that was a good sign. If assassins were waiting for me outside, the dog would at least be barking, wouldn't he? With visions of flying bullets dancing in my head, I half-walked and half-ran out to the garage, making "buk-buk-buk" chicken noises the entire way. Every job has its humiliations.

I had to clear a few boxes and dumbbells from behind the car before I could back it out of the garage. Twenty years ago the Charger had probably been copper, but the paint job had oxidized to something closer to brown. With me in my drab brown clothes, the car and I made a stunning duo.

Turns out the old Dodge looked like a junk pile but drove like a dream come true. Heading out of McGowan's driveway I roared to sixty in seconds flat, recognizing the sweet raucous throttle of a V-8 engine under the hood. I gave the dashboard an approving pat. "Okay, sweetheart, we're partners today." Who would expect such thrills in sheep's clothing? I wondered if good men might be similarly disguised.

I saw by the clock in the Pacific Properties reception area that I had arrived at the perfect hour. By now all the staff had cadged their first cups of coffee and settled in at their desks, but it was probably too early for them to be so engrossed in work that they couldn't be interrupted.

The velvety-voiced young man at the front desk recognized me at once and buzzed Stan. This morning I took a seat on the sofa in the reception area and didn't even fight my reading addiction. I grabbed one of the tempting magazines fanned on the coffee table—a fat, juicy *Vanity Fair*. Alas! No sooner had I opened its glamorous cover than the receptionist called for me to follow him down the hall. I found the interruption highly annoying, probably because it happens to me every week at the checkout lines in the grocery store. I'll see an irresistible headline in an eye-catching tabloid and get in the longest line I can find, hoping to satisfy my inquiring mind's urge to *know*. But by the time I find the damn feature article among all those ads for flatter tummies and "neck" massagers, the cashier is ready for my check. I sometimes fear that this business of life getting in the way of my reading will drive me slowly insane. It's exasperating, an intellectual variation of coitus interruptus. Not that reading about space aliens advising presidents and women giving birth to wolf babies is really all that intellectual.

The receptionist led me to Stan's office. I tapped on the door and heard a voice inside call, "Come in." I turned the knob and pushed gently.

Stan, dressed in tennis shorts, had been sitting on one of the black leather sofas reading *The Wall Street Journal*. He stood up and smiled when I entered the room.

"Hello again, Elizabeth. How is everything going?"

"It's going," I replied. "I've got just a few more questions at this point. Shouldn't take much of your time here."

"Oh, hey, no hurry. As you can see I've got a tennis game coming up, but that's not until ten o'clock, so relax, take your time." He patted my shoulder and resumed his seat. I sat in a matching black chair to his right.

No red aura this morning. He was a lot more at ease than the last time I'd seen him. Even the swaggering was toned down, or maybe the change in clothes had resulted in a corresponding change in attitude.

"Are you making any progress on your investigation?"

"I think so."

"Can you tell me anything about it, or is that stuff confidential at this point?"

"Ah—" I hedged.

"It's just that when you work with someone closely every day, and then you find out that person might have been murdered . . . well, you're concerned, you know?"

"It's probably best that I withhold comment until the case is closed," I said.

"I understand."

"So, Stan, you mentioned that Janice was involved in investor relations—I think you referred to her as a 'talented diplomat,' or words to that effect. Did she by any chance have anything to do with that case that's pending appeal right now, *Pacific Properties III, Limited versus Alexander Spiro?*"

"I only wish she had," he said, emphatically shaking his head. "That whole damn situation was completely avoidable. No, Janice was not a part of it, but I can assure you that if she had been, the lawsuit never would have happened."

He leaned toward me conspiratorially. "This is between you and me, okay? Janice wasn't just ethical—she was smart, too. She advised our managing partner, Alex Spiro, to redistribute that money. But Spiro went off and made one of his bold executive moves. He was convinced the funds could be swept under the 'management fee' clause. What you're reading in the financial news now is the result. A lot of pissed-off investors."

"So Janice had nothing whatsoever to do with that situation?"

"It was completely out of her hands. Any questions people had, she referred them to the attorneys. It had become their feeding frenzy by then."

The blood had risen in his face. "In the great scheme of things, one and a half million doesn't amount to a hill of beans, of course. Sums like that go back and forth between our cash reserves and our investors every quarter. Legally, Pacific Properties is probably in the clear. But as Janice tried to tell people around here, it's that cavalier attitude that gets you in trouble. And it did get this company in trouble. The press we're getting is very negative, and Janice understood how important reputation is. We're really going to miss her around here, I can tell you that."

It sounded good. God knows I wanted to believe him. I could hear a fight starting up between my head and my guts. My head was saying, "Give the guy a break. Listen to him. He's a good guy. He's making sense. He cares."

My gut, on the other hand, was desperately sending up flares. A loud growl rose from my stomach into the silence between Stan and me.

"You hungry? We've got some croissants—"

"No, thank you, I'm fine," I said. Just a little embarrassed, is all.

Stan Ellis picked up the tennis racket propped against the leather sofa and began to inspect the netting. "You play tennis?" he asked.

I shook my head.

"You do something," he said, showing off his little row of very white teeth. "Your body's in great shape."

That was true, but it certainly wasn't evident from the baggy pants and shirt I was wearing today. I thought back to the conservative suit I'd worn here earlier. Not particularly revealing, either. Maybe he was just bullshitting, trying to flatter me.

"How do you stay fit?" he asked.

"Yoga," I said. He look at me quizzically, waiting for an explanation. "I'm not big on competitive sports. I'm fairly coordinated, but I have no killer instinct. Except Scrabble. When I play Scrabble I'm deadly."

"You could take me out, I'm sure," he said with a smile. He glanced at his watch.

"I don't want to keep you, Mr. Ellis, but there is one other thing," I said. "Now this may be kind of a long shot, but do you recognize"—I reached into my purse and pulled out the photo of Michael Huerte—"this man?"

Stan took the photo, peered at it closely, and shook his head. "No, I'm sorry. I don't. Who is he?"

"That's essentially what I'm trying to figure out."

I stopped into the personnel office on my way out. Carrie Aimes was sitting at her desk, a sunflower yellow blazer playing up the drama of her magenta hair. In the lexicon of a fashion designer girlfriend of mine, Carrie was Fashion Forward. She looked up and smiled politely when she saw me at her door.

"Hi, there," she said. "Did Alan Katz ever get back to you?"

"Yes, as a matter of fact."

"How's he doing, anyway?"

"He's pretty shaken up about Janice."

"Aren't we all. So, what else can I do for you?"

I handed her the photo of Huerte and asked, "Has this person ever worked for Pacific Properties?"

She stared into Huerte's face and shook her head. "No, I don't recognize him."

"Not even as one of your maintenance men, a gardener, perhaps?"

"No, I don't think so."

I heard an edge of doubt in her voice. "Carrie, if your life were riding on it—because I have reason to believe that my life is—could you say for a certainty that this man had never had any affiliation with Pacific Properties?"

She caught the seriousness of my question. "Any affiliation? The only thing I can think is an indirect affiliation."

"What do you mean by that?"

"Well, as you may know, Pacific Properties owns buildings all over the West and Hawaii. The way we write our leases, our tenants are responsible for maintenance. What I'm getting to is that it's possible this man could have been employed as a gardener by one of our tenants. A lot of times people pick up Hispanic help along the side of the road. But there's no way you could ever find out. I mean, you'd have to interview the tenants of something like nine hundred properties. Just a second."

She reached into a lower desk drawer and pulled out a thick booklet. "Here's a listing of all the addresses, if you want it."

I took the booklet and fanned the pages. Page after page after page after page of single-spaced addresses made me dizzy. I handed back the book. "Thanks, anyway. I think I'd rather move a truckload of sand with a pair of tweezers, if you know what I mean."

Carrie offered to show me out. We walked down the hall, chatting idly about the artwork. We were nearing the reception area when my antennae unexpectedly went up.

At first I had no idea where the feeling was coming from. Then I noticed a closed door. Something behind it seemed to shout at me. The silent shouting got louder as we approached the closed door.

"What's in here?" I asked, tapping the door with my index finger. Sure enough, I felt something.

Carrie stopped, turned around, and looked at me. "Funny you should ask. That's Janice's old office." She made no move to show me in but continued to usher me down the hall and back out to the reception area. Twice I opened my mouth to request a viewing of the office, but something stopped me each time. I followed Carrie reluctantly, in silence.

When we reached the lobby I shook Carrie's hand and

thanked her for her help. She seemed surprised, pleasantly, by my formality. "Let me know if we can help you with anything else, or if you change your mind and need a copy of our property listings," she said as I walked out.

27

The little bells sang as I walked through the door of Pia Mia's shop. Pia was standing behind the register, talking on the telephone. Today she wore a snug strapless summer dress, her tan skin glowing against the cool white fabric. Her massive mink-brown tresses had been braided with a white ribbon and piled into an elegant heap at the nape of her neck. She waved when she saw me walk in and began to make "gotta go" noises into the phone. As I approached the counter she hung up and said in her throaty voice, "Well, hello there. What a pleasant surprise."

"Told you I'd be back."

She smiled. "What can I do for you today? I just got some darling walk shorts in."

"Unfortunately, I don't have time to shop today. But I wanted to thank you for your help yesterday—not only for the bathing suit, which I love, but also for helping me find that undesirable address, you know, the one behind your shop?"

"Oh, yes. You're welcome." Her eyes twinkled at me. "You're wearing the earrings," she said.

I reached up and grabbed my earlobes. To my surprise I'd completely forgotten about the lapis lazuli earrings. "Oh, they're like a part of me, I swear. Thank you again. Unexpected gifts are always so special."

"Did you get what you were after?"

"Not entirely, I don't think. Tell me something, Pia." I pulled Michael Huerte's picture out of my bag and held it out for her to see. "Does this guy look familiar?"

She glanced at it a moment, then looked up and asked, "Are you a cop?"

"Private investigator."

"Bully for you," she said, a pleased smile crossing her face. "Yeah, that's one of the guys who lives in the back."

"Lived," I corrected. "He's dead now."

"I see."

I then pulled out the most recent picture I had of Janice, the color glossy of her lovely, smiling, half-naked self. "Have you ever seen this woman before?"

Pia took the photo from my hands and stared into it long and hard. "No," she said at last, shaking her head. She looked up at me, her brows arched appreciatively. "But she sure is beautiful."

"You're positive you've never seen her around here anywhere, maybe with some of those people back there?"

She shot me a penetrating glance. "No way. I'd remember her. Believe me, those creeps don't have any girlfriends who look like *that*. Not even close."

"Well, you see, Pia, I'm trying to find out what this guy"—I held out Huerte's picture—"had to do with this woman's death. Nobody seems to be able to tell me much about him. Did you know him at all?"

Pia looked again at Huerte's picture. "Not really."

"Not really but what?"

"Well, this guy was actually okay. We used to run into each other taking out the trash on Wednesdays. He was kind of a ladies' man. Swarthy, but gentle. Heavy on the compliments, but polite. You know the type."

"Did he speak English?"

"Oh, sure. As well as anyone. I thought he was a pretty

decent neighbor, before all those other jerks moved in. Maybe he was hard up for money and had to take what he could for roommates."

"When did the roommates move in?"

"I don't know. A year ago, maybe?"

The bells on the door jamb shimmered. We both looked over and watched a woman wearing a straw hat and carrying a shopping bag walk through the door. She began to sift through some shorts and shirts on a rack near the front of the store. "I'll be with you in a moment," Pia called.

"Other than that I really don't know what to tell you," Pia said to me. She knit her brows. "Maybe you should talk to his landlord."

"You know who that is?"

"Yeah, same landlord I have. The guy owns half this block. Here, let me get you his number."

She flipped through a little Rolodex near the register and pulled out a card. "Here, use this phone."

I waited through seven rings and was about to hang up when the landlord, a guy named Bernie White, finally answered. He sounded old and crotchety but was suddenly quite cooperative when I told him that I was investigating the death of one of his tenants, Michael Huerte. Mr. White was unaware that Huerte had died. That property, he told me, had been leased on a month-to-month basis to Michael Huerte and his brother, José. He said that a while back José Huerte had moved out and Michael had taken on some new roommates.

"Do you know who these people are?" I asked.

"Naw, naw. Huerte always paid his rent right on time, in cash. I don't give a god darn who he choose to live with."

"Mr. White, you wouldn't happen to have the original rental application, would you? Did Michael Huerte list an employer, an alternate address, anything like that?"

"A rental application?" He laughed into the phone. "That's a little fancy for that place, sugar. No, Huerte did occasional odd jobs for me—yard work, hauling, that kind of thing. He was looking for a place to live and seemed like a nice sort, so I let him rent the place. Later he got full-time work for a wealthy family. He was a hard worker, had relatives in Mexico, I think he said—"

"Did Huerte ever mention the name of the family he worked for?"

"Naw, not so I recall."

In the unlikely event Bernie White's memory improved, I gave him McGowan's number at the Escondido Police Department and thanked him for his help.

"Well, golly, that's a shame about Huerte," he said before hanging up the phone. "He was a nice fellow."

I rang off and made a mental list. Property leased month-to-month. Brother José moved out "a while back." New roommates. Full-time work for a wealthy family. Always paid his rent right on time. In cash.

Meanwhile I watched as Pia walked to the front of the store. The white strapless dress hugged her form, laying bare the perfection of her carriage. Pia was a study in beautiful posture. The line from the small of her back to the top of her head was as flawless as that of any Grecian urn. She moved with the fluid grace of a wild animal. She seemed more to float than to take actual steps as she walked through the racks of clothing.

The customer had seen Pia coming and looked up nervously. "Just browsing," I heard her say. She pawed at a few more items before dashing from the store.

"I swear," Pia said turning to me, "I chase customers away."

"Don't take it personally," I said. "Everybody does that. So, you're a dancer, aren't you?"

Pia smiled. "Used to be. Danced with a troupe in San Francisco way back when. Now I'm just an old shopkeeper."

She was kidding, poking fun at herself. "No," I said. "You're still dancing. The way you carry yourself, it looks to me like you'll be dancing through your entire life."

"You trying to bribe another pair of earrings out of me?" I laughed. We both did.

"They do say," Pia said, "that life is but a dance."

"Yes. And some people know all the right steps but have no grace. That, Pia my friend, is not your problem."

"Nor yours," she said kindly.

28

A white Toyota pickup had been making me a little nervous the last few miles. The truck had appeared out of nowhere in my back window and as far as I could tell it was jockeying to catch up with me in the number one lane on northbound Interstate 5. I was now three car lengths in front of him, but I sensed him back there gaining on me as if he were the heat and I were the criminal. Then he began to change lanes to my right. Lane by lane he cut to the opposite side of the freeway. The distance between us lengthened. With a sigh of relief I watched in the rearview as he faded off the interstate two exits south of Rancho Santa Fe.

I had to laugh. "You're not paranoid, Elizabeth," I told myself. "It's just that people are really out to get you." It was true, but I couldn't say it and keep a straight face.

I had the pristine roads of Rancho Santa Fe nearly all to myself this morning. Tom's old Charger, a macho throwback to the sixties, would be affectionately referred to in certain plebeian circles as a "muscle car." I imagine it made an incongruous sight traveling these patrician byways. The car was noisy and fast, and I was madly in love with it as we thundered through orange groves and manicured landscapes. So passionately did I drive that I nearly roared right past the boulder marking the Freeman estate.

I pulled up the driveway and parked next to a white and gold Lexus, so shiny and new it practically blinded me.

Once again I passed the gardener on my way to the front door. One could easily see that it was a full-time job, tending these grounds.

"*Hola, que tal?*" asked as I walked by.

The gardener's deep brown face crinkled warmly as he smiled and replied, "*Bien! Bien! Esta usted?*"

"*Bien, gracias,*" I said with a nod and then proceeded to the front door.

This time it was Paul Freeman who answered the harmonious doorbell. "Hello, there," I said as he swung the door open.

He looked a bit startled to see me but quickly smoothed it over with a polite smile. "Well, my goodness. I was expecting you to telephone. Come in, please." He was dressed in what my fashion savvy friend would call Prosperous Casual. Linen Armani shorts and shirt in subtle earth tones. Together they probably cost more than the best dress hanging in my closet. "It's a little warm for the patio today, Elizabeth. Why don't we sit in the living room?"

The house was blessedly cool. "I wanted to tell you about a call I got yesterday," he continued over his shoulder as we walked into the front room. The square footage in this area alone was adequate for a good-sized apartment. The space managed to feel balanced, though, partly because the furniture was scaled to majestic proportions as well.

"That's a lovely piece," I said, pointing to an antique armoire painted with elongated, saintlike figures. The work looked as if it had been done in tempera, and the style was reminiscent of El Greco.

"Ah, thank you. Sixteenth century. We obtained it from a monastery just outside Rome. I'm rather fond of it myself."

"Ah spotted it first."

Paul and I turned to see Annie standing at the entryway. My first instinct was to make a mad dash for the door, but then I remembered I needed to talk to this lady. She beat me to the punch.

"Ah have to apologize for the other day," she said contritely. "Ah'm back on my medication now. My doctor had to increase the dosage, to take into account the added stress. Ah hope y'all pardon me."

I had to admit she looked a lot better. Her eyes were soft brown, no longer beady. The hair was now a far more believable color—the dark roots had been touched up and the whole thing had been fluffed and smoothed into a sedate coif. The smartly tailored russet suit she wore disguised a whole caboodle of woes.

"I realize I'm here under difficult circumstances," I said.

"Ah'm a depressive," Annie stated frankly. "Ah'm afraid that without my antidepressant medication my behavior gets a little out of hand."

"Thank you for your apology," I said. "I understand completely."

"Ah am especially regretful that ah called you a witch," she added. "That was uncharitable and un-Christian." She didn't look me in the eye when she said it, but at least she'd had the guts to mention it.

"Any gifts I have are the ones God has given me," I said. "I'd like to think I'm using them for the highest good. That's my desire, anyway."

The three of us sat, Paul and Annie taking the intricately carved rosewood sofa while I sank into a divinely comfortable embroidered wing chair.

I turned to Paul. "So, you were telling me you got a call," I began.

"Yes, Alan Katz called me at the office yesterday," he said.

At the mention of Alan's name, Annie didn't sputter and spit as I halfway expected her to, judging from the last time his name had come up. She sat calmly, just listening.

"Why would Alan call you?" I asked Paul.

"I think he just wanted to hear from me that it was true

about Janice's death. Apparently he hadn't known until he heard it from you."

"Well, did he shed any light on what might have happened?"

"No." Paul shook his head. "He seemed to be quite in the dark."

I put on a thoughtful expression, but in actuality I was studying Paul Freeman. It was easy to see where Janice had gotten her good looks. Mr. Freeman's recent grief hadn't ravaged his handsome face, and time had silvered—not grayed—his lustrous hair.

"Yet you called me. Was there something else?" I asked after a lengthy pause.

"I just wanted to tell you that given the tone of his phone call—the boy was really quite broken up—I don't think he could have at all been responsible for Janice. I honestly don't."

"What about you?" I said, turning to Annie. "You had fairly strong feelings about this the last I heard."

"Ah was exaggeratin'. Alan Katz is a loser. He fathered a child out of wedlock, you know." She gave me this last tidbit in a tone that assumed I'd be both titillated and mortified. "But ah suppose he's not a murderer. It's just that ah always figured Janice to be above his station."

It was time to drop a bomb and watch faces, to see who did or didn't look surprised. "Someone tried to kill me last night, you know," I said.

Paul's alarm was palpable, but was Annie's startled look genuine? I couldn't tell. "Good Lord!" "Well for heaven's sakes, who?" the pair of them burst out simultaneously.

"I didn't get a real good look." Well, it was true. Let them think I caught a peek.

Paul Freeman leaned toward me with obvious concern. "Shouldn't the police be handling this, then, at this point?"

"They're working on it," I said reassuringly. I myself was not so reassured. Then again, my expectations of the police department were probably too high. After all, a police report had been filed. That's work, right?

After shock, my next agenda item was show-and-tell. I pulled Huerte's picture from my purse, noticing that it was getting a little ragged at the edges. "Have either of you ever seen this man?"

They leaned forward and pored conscientiously over the photo. "I certainly don't recognize him," Paul said, slowly shaking his head.

"Can't say as ah do either," Annie said.

"Who is he?" Paul asked.

"This was the other victim in Janice's accident," I replied.

At that they both leaned closer with morbid curiosity. "Oh, my," Annie said under her breath, tsking softly.

It occurred to me to ask Annie if she was one of those miserly heiresses who did insane things like clip coupons and shop garage sales and murder only daughters so they could inherit their husbands' entire fortune. I couldn't find the appropriate opening, somehow.

"Well, I guess that's about all I have for now." I put away the photo and stood to go.

"Sorry we couldn't be of more help," Paul said as he and Annie showed me toward the front door. On our way through the gallery I stopped to admire a picture in a silver frame sitting on a black grand piano. In perfect black-and-white profile, Janice—ever photogenic—stared hopefully at some far-off destination.

"Why don't ya'll take that?" Annie said.

"Oh, no—"

She snatched up the frame and placed it in my hands. "Ah insist thatcha do. We have another copy, don't we, Paul? It's the least ah can do, after the other day."

"Thank you," was all I could think to say.

As they stood in the doorway—the trim, distinguished West Coast executive and the amply fleshed Southern heiress—I took a mental picture and again pondered the unlikely coupling.

On my way out through the grounds I stepped off the pathway and walked over to the gardener. He was working on his knees in a flower bed under the shade of a massive eucalyptus tree, planting clumps of deep blue lobelia. He squinted into the sun as he looked up at me.

"*Pardon,*" I said, kneeling alongside him with the picture of Huerte. "*Conoce a este hombre?*" I asked, pointing to the photo. Do you know this man?

He looked carefully at the picture. He seemed to be one of the few people who recognized—and were taken aback by—the mask of death.

"*No,*" he said, shaking his head. "*Dispensa, no conosco a este persona.*" Damn.

It would have been a long shot, but Huerte's landlord had said he'd gone to work for a wealthy family. Apparently not the Freemans, though.

"*Gracias,*" I said with a sigh.

29

I felt the beginnings of a demoralization attack coming on. Things weren't happening. The obscure was not becoming clear; the pieces were not falling into place. As far as I could tell I'd managed to accomplish virtually nothing on this case, except to put my life in danger. What was it the World's Most Famous Psychic, Lenny Lenton, had said? Some bullshit about a positive attitude. Maybe I needed to call a psychic hotline. I could hear Linda giggling in my mind. It was about the twentieth time she'd crossed my thoughts today. Then came a bright idea: Call Linda.

I pulled into a gas station outside of Rancho Santa Fe. The Charger undeniably had a terrible thirst for gasoline. I filled the tank and then dialed Linda's home phone number from a pay phone at the side of station.

"Hel-lo."

God, I loved her voice. Her voice alone was probably worth $3.99 a minute.

"Hey, Lind, it's me."

"You got my message."

"No. I haven't been home for the last day or so. I, uh, needed to get away for a while. When did you call?"

"I didn't say I called," she giggled. "I said you got my message. I've been sending you thought forms. You obviously picked up on them. So tell me about the trouble you're in."

"Why don't I meet you somewhere?"

"Oh, dear," she said direly. "I don't like the sound of your voice. At all."

"How about Kung Food in half an hour? I'm buying."

Linda was holding down a table in the outside dining area of Kung Food, a culinary haven for vegetarians. She sat in the shade of a jasmine-covered trellis, looking regal as always. Somehow Linda finds these fabulous flowing garments in sumptuous colors that never fade and never need ironing. Or maybe she just imbues her raiment with her own radiant hues. She is large and handsome and looks like she belongs to another time, when women were the power and the wisdom and the glory. Her presence is at once commanding and mysterious. I have never known her to be unkind.

She stood up as I approached and took me into her arms, filling me up with her generous love.

"Ahh," I purred.

"Hmm," she said, holding me at arm's length and appraising me. She made little tsking noises. "A little fearful energy around you, eh? Sit down; I'll clear you."

We took our seats, and Linda closed her eyes. She took a loud, deep breath and exhaled noisily. I watched her face. She took another deep breath, and another. As she worked I could feel the energy moving, as if the very molecules that surrounded us were beginning to dance. I closed my eyes and saw colors blending and separating around me. For the first time all day I felt sensations approaching peacefulness, warmth, and comfort. Life was good again.

Our waitress, a petite brunette who wore her hair in two long, thick braids, approached our table. This being the type of vegetarian restaurant where metaphysicians hang out, a woman in trance at the table was 'no big.' In deference to Linda's meditation, our waitress leaned over me, braids swaying, and spoke softly. "What can I get for you here?"

"Chamomile tea and a honey-nut muffin," Linda said joyously without opening her eyes.

"Make it a double," I said.

After several minutes Linda opened her eyes. "Right now, Elizabeth, I recommend about ten doses of white light an hour. You are in some deep shit, honey."

"Thanks for the vote of confidence."

She shrugged that one off. "What do you want me to do, my dear, lie to you?"

"No. Help me. I'm stuck."

"There's a man and a building," she said. "The building is large, like a cathedral, but not a cathedral. It looks unfinished, as if it's still being built."

"The California Center for the Arts."

Linda paused, shrugged, and went on. "The man has a key for you. Now this is a vision, so the key could be anything. I think it's safe to say the man has something to help you get unstuck."

"Alan Katz."

Linda took a drink from her water glass. "Now, there's another man. He looks bigger than life, like Paul Bunyan. He's also there to help. I don't know, he could be an angel, or a guide. His aura is almost white, and he's very statuesque."

"Oh, him? He's definitely an angel."

I pulled the silver-framed picture of Janice from my purse. "What about her?" I asked.

Linda smiled as she held the picture in her hands. She was quiet for a minute. Once or twice she chuckled and nodded. "This is the girl who died?" she asked.

"Uh-huh."

"She's very happy with you. She wants to help you. You're on the right track, she says."

"I'm totally lost."

"No, you're not. You're getting there." Linda was silent

again. "Oh," she said, startled. "She wants you to give her love, her understanding, to the man with the key."

"Alan."

"Yes. Alan."

30

I drove past the Center for the Arts on the way back to McGowan's that evening, in the hope that some of the construction crew might still be lingering about. But it was past five, and there were no signs of life at the site. The frame of the building-in-progress stood empty and silent. Silhouetted against the setting sun, it looked like the gigantic skeleton of some postmodern beast.

McGowan's cruiser was not in the driveway when I drove in. I pulled the Charger into the garage. Contained in four walls, the engine made a deafening commotion. As soon as I turned off the ignition I could hear Nero inside, barking frantically. I sure hoped the hound would remember me fondly. Loudly, I made nice-doggie noises as I put the key in the lock. But Nero had an excellent memory. He greeted me with wild enthusiasm, leaping toward me and then pulling himself back, as if he knew restraint was appropriate here but just couldn't help himself.

Other than Nero's happy panting, the house was very quiet. I hadn't talked to McGowan all day. I felt a little pang of disappointment now and realized I'd assumed I'd see him for dinner. I wandered into the kitchen and found another note on the table.

If you're reading this, good job, you didn't get your butt killed today. Rodney had a family emergency. I'm taking his swing

shift. Orange roughy and lemon wedges in refrigerator, HBO
on cable. See you eleven-thirtyish. Try to behave. T

The note went a long way toward assuaging my blues.
The orange roughy, too, did quite a bit to cheer me. It
broiled up into a feather-light, ambrosia-from-the-sea type
of entrée, the kind of dish I'd never prepare for myself at
home. The meal was wonderful, but I couldn't shake the
loneliness. My mood was serious, and I needed a serious
cure. Times like these are what bubble baths are all about.
Knowing McGowan, I wouldn't be surprised to find a variety of salts and perfumed oils in the guest bathroom.

I put my dishes in the dishwasher—something else I
probably wouldn't bother to do at home on any given week-
night. That completed, I padded back to the bathroom.
There, standing in the bathroom doorway, I had an ugly
shock.

It was everywhere. All over the sink. All over the shower
curtain. All over the towels. Even the floor was covered. Everywhere I looked: panty hose. Gasping for breath, I cleared
the filmy stockings from the room like an arachnophobic
sweeping away spiderwebs. Where McGowan got so many
pairs of the damn things I could only wonder. This was his
way of extracting my penance, of course, for leaving his toilet seats up. I really hadn't thought he'd even notice.

When the room was finally safe, I ran hot water in the
bathtub. Sure enough, there were Epsom salts under the
sink. I sank into the warm liquid heaven and spent the next
twenty minutes doing my own version of rebirthing. I
emerged from the womb with no trauma whatsoever.

It hadn't occurred to me to pack nighties, so I was
forced—really—to borrow without asking. I went into
McGowan's closet and found a fire-hydrant-yellow T-shirt
with POLICE in large, black lettering across the back. I
slipped it on and checked it out in the bathroom mirror. On

me it was tunic length. One hundred percent cotton, V-neck, totally cool. Poor McGowan would never see this thing again. I wondered what I might have that I could trade. Maybe I could read his horoscope or something.

I lay down on the sofa with the intention of meditating, thinking about the case, something constructive. But my mind was weary and I soon dropped into a restless sleep. The dreaming began in the ordinary, nonsensical way dreams often do. I remember something about needing to hurry along to the dry cleaners or else I wouldn't have the right clothes to wear for some big celebration somewhere. The lady behind the counter at the cleaners told me I would have to wait out back for my clothes. She showed me through a door and down a long hallway. There was a cot along the side of the hallway and she told me to stay there. I lay down on the cot, not questioning her odd request, the way we often accept the bizarre in our dreams.

Then the frozen feeling came over me. It's a sleep-state phenomenon that happens to me from time to time. I'm not really asleep or awake, but stuck in limbo between the two. I had somehow stepped outside the dream, that was clear. Yet I was not moving into another dream, nor was I falling deeper into imageless sleep, nor was I waking up. I was just stuck.

I knew I must find the hallway again. And with that thought I was back in the dream, walking down the hallway. I saw my body on the cot. A crowd had gathered around. The people were all looking at me and commenting on how perfectly preserved I appeared to be and how strange it was that no flies or worms had infested my body, even though it had been weeks since I'd died. I had the feeling of desperately wanting to break through the surface of this dream, to move, to wake up—much like the urgency you feel when you're swimming up from deep waters and your life depends on getting a breath of air.

I woke up with a start to see McGowan's face leaning over me, just inches away. His hand was resting on my shoulder.

"I had a bad dream," I said groggily. "I was dreaming I was dead and couldn't wake up."

He didn't say anything but came close and put his mouth against mine. His lips were warm and comforting and oddly familiar. Then he began to kiss me in earnest, the kind of kissing you feel from your head to your toes, but mostly about halfway in between. The dream was quickly banished. I now had no doubt that my body was alive and well. McGowan slid his hands under the T-shirt and along my sides, a move that met with wild approval from my autonomous nervous system. His exploration of my thighs, too, got an excellent reception. My hands became incredibly curious as to what they might find under *his* shirt. It went on like this for some time, one thrilling discovery after another.

"Tom," I said, pulling away from his lips for a moment, my hands still wrapped around his neck, "does that well-stocked guest bath of yours house any condoms of recent vintage?"

He made a "hmm" noise and reached for the police belt I'd removed only moments ago. It was one of those bulky jobs with a million compartments.

"I keep all my life-saving stuff in here," he said. He unsnapped a little leather flap at the front of the belt and pulled out a small can. "Mace," he identified. He reached into the leather holster at the side of the belt and pulled out his piece. "Revolver." He unsnapped still another compartment at the back of the belt and pulled out a pair of metal bracelets. "Handcuffs," he said, placing them into my hands. With dancing eyebrows he added, "We can use those, too."

I laughed.

"Just kidding." He smiled, still probing the belt's secret compartments.

"Ah-ha," he said at last, holding aloft a small, square, foil packet.

I was in the hallway again. I found the cot, but it was empty. I looked down the hallway and saw Janice, her blonde hair shinier than in her pictures, her animated face more beautiful. She was standing at the end of the hallway, waiting for me. She waved me toward her.

I began walking. As I drew nearer to Janice I somehow knew we were in the hallway of the Pacific Properties building. We walked to the door of Janice's office. She took out a key and opened it. I followed her inside. She walked to her desk on the left side of the room, near the window. She reached into her top desk drawer and pulled out a file folder. She turned around and looked at me intently. She placed the folder in my hands and said, "This is it." Then she was on the phone, the receiver cradled against her neck. She wrote something on a piece of paper and handed it to me. I looked at her note and tried to read it, but it seemed to be written in another language. Then I recognized that it wasn't a language at all, but numbers.

I heard a loud slam and woke with a start. I was in McGowan's big bed, but he wasn't. The sound had come from the master bathroom.

"What was that?" I called out.

"I was putting the toilet seat down. Didn't mean to wake you. Sorry."

McGowan appeared in the bathroom doorway. He was surrounded by a faint white glow.

"What an angel you are," I said.

31

True, I thought. McGowan had worked two shifts back to back. Still, there was something obscene in the way he was so thoroughly gone to the world. For the last hour or so I'd been watching the steady rise and fall of his chest under the sheets. It didn't seem quite fair. I had slept fitfully all night. Part of this I chalked up to the novelty of sleeping with an actual human being. It had been some time since I'd last done this sort of thing, after all. But most of my restlessness came from within. After dreaming of Janice I felt anxious to return to her office. But before that could happen, I knew, I would have to find that key Linda had told me about yesterday.

When dawn at last fully entered the bedroom and shadows began to take on a faint bit of color, I gave up on the idea of lounging around for possible morning lovemaking. Staring down at McGowan's herculean form I found it hard to believe, but my mind was already elsewhere. Still, it did take some effort to pull away from him, the way a satellite needs a little booster to break from the pull of a planet's gravity.

It was my turn to leave a note. *Early bird gets the vermin*, I wrote. Not terribly sentimental, but then I've never done my best work in the morning. *Love your gun*, I added, in what I hoped would be a comforting addendum.

As luck would have it, construction workers start early. I

revved up the Charger and headed into downtown Escondido well ahead of the eight o'clock rush. I drove into the heart of the city, where the California Center for the Arts would eventually occupy an entire block adjacent to city hall. At the moment the cultural mecca-to-be was just a pile of steel girders and the beginnings of architectural details like triangular roofs and rounded corners. For the last several weeks I'd watched it slowly rising out of mounds of cleared earth, a dreamer awakening.

I parked along the street and wondered what to do next. I got out of the car. It was another hot morning, and instantly I regretted my black pants and shirt. The sounds of jackhammers and buzz saws filled the air. Men wearing equipment belts stood along the rising framework and milled around the cement foundation. I approached a man who was leaning against an outside wall frame, eating a doughnut.

"Looking for a guy named Alan Katz," I said.

The man nodded. "You his girlfriend?"

I shook my head.

"You wanna be my girlfriend?"

I smiled, no comment. He smiled back and said, "Just a second and I'll go get him."

I watched him walk up a half-finished stairwell to a second floor wide open to the sky. He walked perhaps another fifty paces to the corner of the huge building, where I could see him talking to a group of coworkers. Then he turned to me and waved. "C'mon over here!" he called.

I followed along the edge of the building from ground level. The ground was uneven. Unstable dirt clumps gave way beneath my feet, making the going rough. I did my best not to stumble. When I got about halfway there, the catcalls started. Primal sounds. Something like the yipping of coyotes on a moonlit night, only more guttural. I thought decency would quiet the pack as I approached, but if anything the noise escalated as I drew nearer.

When I was directly beneath the assembled workers I put my hands on my hips and stared into their faces. They all looked like nice enough people. "Why do you guys do that?" I asked.

Alan stepped out from the back of the group. "I told you, Elizabeth, you're a knockout," he called down.

"No, really," I said to the assembled men. "What compels you to yelp like wild animals when a woman walks by?"

"I think it's because we're wild animals," one of them said. Several heads nodded and I heard a few "yeps" and a "definitely" or two. I accepted these comments at face value.

"I need to talk to you, Alan," I said. "Alone, if I could."

At that, a pandemonium of whooping and howling broke out among the pack. "I'll be right down," he said, his words barely audible above the raucous chorus.

We walked across the lot and sat on the cement foundation in a relatively empty area of the construction site. "You're the man with the key," I said to him.

"The key?"

"The key to Janice's murder. By the way, she sends her regards."

He looked at me sideways. "It's funny you say that."

"Why?"

"Because remember what you were telling me the other night, about forgiveness and all? I, um . . . I felt too silly actually to talk to Janice, but I did write her a letter telling her I was . . . you know, how sorry I was about what happened between us. I don't know about Janice at this point, but I feel a lot better. A *lot* better."

Should I tell him about Linda's message from Janice? Perhaps obliquely. "I think Janice got the message," I said.

Alan was wearing a bright yellow hard hat, and his red hair curled out from under it onto the collar of his blue work shirt. "Aren't you hot in that hat?" I had to ask.

He turned and smiled at me, his dimples melting the

sharp corners in my edgy mood. "What, this? Believe it or not I don't mind the hat nearly so much as these." He held out his feet. He was wearing industrial-strength construction boots, boots that looked as if they could withstand a hike or two through hell. "I wouldn't be without either of them, though. This occupation has some deadly hazards."

"Yes," I mused. "So does mine, I'm discovering."

"Hell, yeah. You're bound to piss people off, doing what you're doing."

"As Janice did, apparently."

He looked puzzled. "Do you think? I'm trying to figure that out. I wish I could help you."

"You can," I said. "You are the key. What do you know that I don't? Talk to me. Let's talk about the women in Janice's life. What about her stepmother? Off the top of your head, would you say that Lou Ann Freeman is the type of person who would off her stepdaughter for money?"

"Who, Lou Ann?" Alan took off his hard hat and laughed good-naturedly. He ran his fingers through his damp red curls. "No. Lou Ann is just stupid, not evil."

"She doesn't seem to like you very much. It seems she has some questions about your family values."

Alan leaned back and had himself a good laugh. "Family values? Baloney. That's not it. Did I ever tell you about the first time we met? Janice had me to her parents' house for dinner. When Janice introduced us Lou Ann turned to me and said, 'Katz. That's an interesting name. Is that C as in *cat*, or K as in *kike?*' She hates me because I'm Jewish."

"Well, that too maybe. You mentioned you have a daughter by an ex-girlfriend. Tell me about her."

His eyes lit up. "She's adorable."

"Not your daughter. Your ex. Is her name Tanya?"

"Yes. Why do you ask?"

"I'm wondering if Tanya knew Janice, or had any reason to hate her."

Alan made a "shhshh" noise and said, "She was certainly

no great fan of Janice's, but I can't exactly see Tanya killing her. Saying she wanted to, maybe, but actually doing it? No way."

"So Tanya knew Janice?"

"More like knew *of* her. I started seeing Janice about the time I broke it off once and for all with Tanya."

"Tanya hated Janice's guts, in other words."

"Yeah, but I can't see Tanya masterminding a car accident. Forget it. No way. She's really more bark than bite. You'd see if you met her."

I pictured the Tanya I remembered from my trip to Ramona, smoking her bhang and snarling at me in her New Jersey accent.

"I've met her. It's a hell of a bark."

"Nah. Tanya's harmless. She was upset for a while there but she got over it, really."

I wasn't so sure.

"Let's talk about Pacific Properties," I continued. "Tell me again about your life there. When you started, what you did, why you left."

Alan paused and looked genuinely puzzled. "Can I ask why you think it's me who's the key to this thing?"

"Never mind, just talk. Ramble on and don't even worry about what might or might not be relevant. Let me be the judge of that. Come on. Pacific Properties."

"Okay, I moved over here from Hawaii in January of ninety-one. Fell crazy in love with Janice. Was doing lots of drugs. I tried to keep that from Janice, but I started blowing it. Got high with Janice's boss once, which probably didn't help—"

"You got high with Stan Ellis?"

"Yeah. Not very cool, huh?"

I thought back to the first time I'd asked Stan Ellis about Alan. The way Stan had pretended not to know Alan. The way he'd averted his eyes from mine, searching for some bullshit answer.

"When did you get high with Stan Ellis?" I asked.

"At one of the Pacific Properties shindigs. We smoked a doobie outside, and he asked me if I knew where he could score some blow. I don't know, I thought he was cool. I put him together with a guy I knew in PB—"

"A guy in Pacific Beach? What was his name?"

"Jay."

"Jay who?"

"I don't even know his last name."

"Frizzy hair?"

Alan looked at me in surprise. "You know him?"

My heart was starting to pound. I felt an urgent need to think. Someone was calling Alan back to the work site. Alan looked over. "Hey, I gotta get going," he said.

"Just a minute, Alan, just a minute. How long after you put Stan together with Jay did you lose your job?"

"Oh, God. I don't know. A month, two—it's hard to remember. My head was pretty fuzzy back then. Why? Does it matter?"

"Did Stan know you were seeing Janice?"

"Hell, yeah. Everybody knew."

Stan had pretended not to know. Another lie. Why would Stan lead an investigator to believe he had no awareness of Alan Katz, or of Alan's relationship with Janice Freeman?

"Why do you think you were fired?"

Alan kicked at the dirt. "I was a fuck-up. I was doing drugs and sleeping with Stan's star employee."

"But Stan Ellis did drugs, too. So why should he care if you partied now and again? How much was it really affecting your work? Enough to lose your job over?"

Some earnest calls were summoning Alan back to the work site. "I gotta go, man," he said.

"Do you think Carrie Aimes, the personnel lady at Pacific Properties, will shed any light on this for me?"

"I don't know," he said, getting up and dusting off his

pants. "But tell her I said hi, okay? I'll talk to you later. Maybe we can have dinner or something." He gave me an apologetic smile and turned to go.

I watched Alan walk. The shoulder-to-buns ratio was sensational, and his rhythmic stride showed it off in a way that mesmerized. Quite philosophically, I wondered why my deep appreciation of his virility did not yet compel me to whoop and holler. Nature or nurture?

32

"Me again."

I smiled and waved at the receptionist. "Oh, hi," he said, all dulcet tones and civilized mien. "Were you wanting to talk to Mr. Ellis again?"

"No. Carrie Aimes. I think she's expecting me."

Before driving down to San Diego, I'd called and left a message on Carrie's voice mail, telling her I'd changed my mind and wanted a copy of that booklet of Pacific Properties's property listings after all.

"Carrie Aimes is in the process of interviewing right now," he said. "But I'll call her and tell her you're here."

Once again I sat on the leather sofa in front of the magazine display. Their brightly colored covers didn't entice me today. My mind was crowded with news, scandals, and speculations of its own. I stared at the ocean and thought about my game plan.

"It's going to be a while," the receptionist said, hanging up the phone. "Can you wait?"

"I can."

I can sit here and ponder, I thought. For some reason Stan had wanted Alan out of this office. Stan had wanted Janice out, too, but there were no easy grounds for dismissal. Alan had been removed before he could become a problem. But Janice had lingered long enough to discover something that had cost her her life.

A woman appeared from the back hallway. Professionally, she was dressed to the nines: navy blue suit, understated jewelry, sensible but expensive matching pumps. Without a word to anyone she walked across the lobby and out the front door. She had worn the dejected look of someone who'd just bombed a job interview. A moment later the man at the reception desk called over to me, "Carrie can see you now." He rose to escort me to her office.

When I walked in, Carrie Aimes was returning some papers to a file. "Sorry about the wait. We're interviewing— for Janice's replacement, as a matter of fact."

"How's it going?"

"She's a hard person to replace. Stan said something about you being a psychic investigator? That's wild."

"Wild? Yes. It's had its wild moments of late."

"So you're going to investigate over nine hundred places to see if the man in that picture ever worked at a location owned by Pacific Properties?" Carrie was searching her desk for the booklet of property listings. "I don't get it. Why do you think the drunk who ran into Janice had anything to do with our company?"

A good question. There was definitely a brain under that magenta hair.

"I'm not really free to discuss the particulars of the case just now," I said lamely.

"Investigating all these properties will take forever." She handed me the booklet across the desk.

"Maybe I'll hire nine hundred friends to help me and we'll do it in a day."

"Good idea. I would if I were you." She laughed in a way I could tell she didn't give a rat's behind what I did with my time, my booklet, or my friends.

"By the way, Alan Katz sends his regards," I said. I was beginning to feel like a messenger of regards.

"Poor Alan," she sighed. "How's he doing?"

"I think he's doing just fine. There is life after Pacific Properties, you know."

"Oh, yeah?" Carrie replied. "Tell that to Janice Freeman." She quickly put her hand over her mouth. "Oh, God, bad joke. Sorry."

The phone on her desk rang before I could respond. "Hello? Oh, hello, Mr. Spiro," Carrie said in a subservient voice.

This was obviously an important call. I saw the opportunity and ran with it. Catching Carrie's eye, I pointed toward the door and mouthed, "Thank you. I'm going. Bye." I gave a little wave and saw myself out of her office.

I stood in the hallway and felt my adrenaline begin to flow. A man in glasses came around the corner; we nodded to each other silently as he walked by. When he disappeared through the end of the hallway I hurried to Janice's door. It was closed, but the knob turned. I slipped inside and closed the door.

The room looked vaguely as it had in my dream. The desk and the file cabinet were there, but on different walls, as if my dream had turned the room backward or inside out. The office appeared abandoned. Most of Janice's personal effects had been packed up. Several bankers' boxes filled with books and accessories lined the far wall. I walked to the desk and pulled open the top drawer. The file was in the exact place from which I'd seen Janice retrieve it in my dream. I didn't even pause to review its contents but simply slipped it into my oversized bag.

I leafed through the day-by-day calendar on her desk, not knowing what to look for. There were names and numbers on practically every page. I felt a little panicky, the way you feel when you're stumped on a multiple-choice test. You have to choose something, but what? The calendar, too, found its way into my purse.

A single frame from my dream appeared in my mind: Janice on the phone.

I looked at the phone on her desk. It was the console variety, with a quartz display panel at the top. I picked up the receiver and hit the redial button, to see what number Janice had called last. A seven-digit number appeared on the panel at the top of the phone. I found a pen and scribbled the number onto a piece of paper and slipped it into my pocket. Next I stepped away from the desk and walked toward the file cabinet.

"What are you doing in here?"

I turned to see Stan and Carrie standing in the doorway. They'd been sneaky about it—I hadn't heard the door open.

"I'm sorry," I said respectfully, in my best kiss-ass voice. You could practically hear me wringing my little hands. "I know I should've asked first before coming in here. But Carrie was on the phone, and I really just wanted to stand in Janice Freeman's space and see if I could pick up on her energy."

Carrie and Stan exchanged amused looks.

"You see, this office would be the best place to pick up on Janice's vibes," I prattled on. I hoped I appeared as truly ridiculous as I sounded.

Stan smirked and said, "Vibes or no vibes, Miss—"

"Chase."

"Miss Chase, Pacific Properties is a securities firm. There's a lot of confidential financial information in this office. Now, I'm afraid we can't just leave unauthorized people hanging around without supervision. It's like what I was talking about to you earlier. We have a reputation to uphold. You understand, I'm sure."

"Yeah, I understand. Besides," I said, giving the best New Age bimbette rendition I could muster, "Janice's spirit has passed on. She's gone to the light, y'know?"

33

All that bad acting at Janice's old office had worked up quite an appetite in me, so I stopped at a Mexican restaurant for a breakfast burrito. I know it's un-American, but the smell of bacon and eggs in the morning has always made me vaguely queasy. The aroma of fresh baked tortillas, salsa, and cilantro, on the other hand, appeals to me no matter what time of day it is. Authentic Mexican burritos—not the plasticized American variety—are juicy and a bit unwieldy. When I had my burrito firmly under control, I spread the items I'd pilfered from Janice's office onto the table in front of me.

The contents of the file I'd pulled from the desk drawer were less than exciting. There was a four-by-six color photograph of a fast-food restaurant, a lease agreement, a title deed, and a copy of a check for $9,500 made out to Pacific Properties and dated June 1. The account printed on the check read "Family Restaurants, Inc." and a handwritten notation below said, "June rental payment." This all looked like pretty standard stuff for the contents of a real estate investment firm file. I did notice a coincidence, though: The photograph depicted a Royal Burger restaurant, the same company Janice's father presided over. I looked at the title deed again. The address was listed as 150 Main Street, Ramona, California. *Ramona.* That just might qualify as another coincidence. I leafed through the booklet of property listings, to cross-check the Ramona address. Sure enough, there it was.

On a whim, I found a pay phone at the back of the restaurant and called Janice's father at the Royal Burger corporate headquarters. He was in the office this morning, and his secretary put me through.

"Just a couple of quick questions, Mr. Freeman. Royal Burger is a very large chain, I realize—"

"Six thousand restaurants nationwide, ten thousand worldwide."

"Now, how are these properties owned? Are they all franchises, or—"

"About thirty-five percent are franchised, but sixty-five percent are corporately owned. We're very selective in terms of whom we allow to use the Royal Burger name."

"Well, given that there are ten thousand Royal Burgers worldwide, I don't expect you to be intimately familiar with every outlet. But I'm wondering if you can tell me anything about a Royal Burger up in Ramona. Does that one happen to be franchised to a Family Restaurants, Incorporated?"

"It's very strange that you're asking me this question, Elizabeth."

"Why so?"

"Janice asked me the same thing the week before she died."

Silence on both ends of the line.

"And," Paul Freeman continued, "I'll tell you exactly what I told Janice. We do have an outlet in Ramona, and it's corporately owned by Royal Burger. I don't know of any Family Restaurants, Incorporated."

I leafed through the paperwork again. "Bear with me a minute here," I said.

"Take your time," he replied kindly.

The lease agreement named Pacific Properties as the owner and Family Restaurants as the tenant. I scrutinized the title deed. It clearly stated that the property was owned by Pacific Properties. "Mr. Freeman," I said, "there seems to be a mistake. Pacific Properties holds the title on this property."

"No, I double-checked that for Janice. There's a mistake somewhere."

"Or no mistake at all," I said. "Thanks for your help."

Next I called the number that had flashed onto Janice's telephone console when I'd hit her redial button. This could be something or nothing. In any event, explaining my call would be tricky. I was thinking up possible lead-ins when a voice came on the line.

"San Diego Police Department, Vice."

A woman's voice, terse, harried. For a moment I was speechless.

"Hello?"

"Yes," I answered quickly, "with whom am I speaking?"

"Detective Reynolds."

"Detective Reynolds, I'm calling with regard to a matter involving Janice Freeman."

"Who's this?"

"My name is Elizabeth Chase. I'm investigating Janice Freeman's death. I know she was in contact with you recently. I wondered if we might meet to discuss this matter."

"I'll be frank with you, Chase. The name Janice Freeman rings a bell but I'm not sure why. You say this woman's deceased?"

"Yes."

"I'm going to have to look at my phone log and get back to you. You got a number?"

"How about I meet you in half an hour? This is very important."

Reynolds hesitated. "All right," she said after a long pause.

* * *

Once upon a time the San Diego Police Department occupied a grand old station on Harbor Drive, with a view of seafaring vessels and the deep blue bay. By the 1980s land values had shot up as fast and high as crime rates, and the department on the waterfront found itself neither economically nor strategically located. Today the PD is housed in a seven-story block of blue glass and gray cement on the southeastern corner of downtown San Diego. It's farther from the water but closer to the action. Inside, it's an endless warren of rooms and passageways, an urban spelunker's paradise.

I sat with Detective Reynolds in the dim light of one of the department's stucco caves, trying to piece together the last days of Janice's life. Reynolds was an extremely physically fit cop in her thirties, with short blonde hair and sharp blue eyes. My attempts to warm her to me with my scintillating humor had met with all the success of feeble matches tossed onto wet logs. I tried not to take it personally. The woman had probably been born without the ability to sense irony, the way some people are born without the ability to curl their tongues. I tried not to curl mine at her now.

Reynolds's phone log had shown no record of a call from Janice Freeman. But I'd leafed through Janice's day-at-a-glance calendar and found an appointment with Reynolds penned in for 2:00 P.M. on June 8, the day after Janice died.

"You didn't think it strange that she'd missed the appointment?" I asked.

"Let me tell you how it is," Reynolds said rigidly. "Joe Citizen wants to see a cop about his suspicion of some illegal activity going on somewhere. There are a lot of nut cases out there, Chase. Maybe their gripe is legitimate, very often it's not. We're polite, we follow up on all our calls, but we don't panic if someone makes an appointment and never shows. It happens all the time."

"So you have no record of what Janice Freeman might have been calling on you about."

"Again, no. I don't. Sorry."

"But if you had to guess?"

Reynolds shrugged. "God only knows. This is Vice. Her call got put through to this department for one of five reasons—prostitution, alcohol, tobacco, firearms, drugs."

"What about illicit financial activity?" I asked, leafing again through the Pacific Properties file. The $9,500 check was beginning to look irregular to me.

"No. Business fraud is handled by the Business Department. If the deceased got put through to me, my guess is she was calling about hooking or drugging, one of the two. Maybe both."

I thanked Reynolds for her time and told her I could see my way out. Big mistake. My standard extrasensory equipment does not include radar. I made a few senseless loops through the labyrinthine offices and found my way out only by following a pair of uniforms heading out for coffee.

Filling the Charger's gas tank seemed to take an eternity. I felt a bead of sweat trickle down my belly as I stood at the unshaded pump of the Ramona Arco station. At last the gas pump handle snapped shut. I nearly emptied my wallet paying the cashier.

The Royal Burger wasn't hard to find. It was one of three food establishments in Ramona's tiny downtown. I walked through the doors and for a change welcomed the refrigeration of air conditioning. Ordinarily I love the heat and loathe canned air, but the weather we'd been having was thick and muggy, not the light, dry heat a desert dweller like me is accustomed to. The humidity seemed to be building in intensity as the week wore on. Today it was practically unbearable. I hoped something would break soon.

Business was slow, to say the least. I was the only customer in the place. A boy-man, someone who would have to show ID before purchasing alcohol, stood in the kitchen area. "Hi," I called to him. "May I speak with the manager, please?"

"I'm the assistant manager, ma'am. You can speak to me."

Is it just me, or is "ma'am" as offensive as all get-out? I know it's meant to be respectful, but every time I'm addressed as "ma'am" I feel I'm being relegated to some dump heap for outworn females. And why is it that "sir" (*"Yes, sir!"*) doesn't carry the same frumpy connotation?

I thought these thoughts and tried not to resent the young man. I hoped that by the time he was twenty-two a girlfriend or lover would clue him in. "I wonder if I could ask a few questions about your business here," I said. "Apparently there's some confusion regarding the title to this property."

"Sure, I can answer any questions you have," he said eagerly. Fortunately for me the kid was insecure about his age, or lack of it. In an effort to impress me with his knowledge he laid bare the facts without an iota of sensitivity to the privacy of the restaurant's financial affairs. He never even asked me whom I worked for.

We settled into one of the empty booths and agreed that the photograph was indeed an image of the very restaurant in which we were sitting. He looked at the title deed and expressed his absolute unfamiliarity with the document. He looked, too, at the $9,500 check and whistled low under his breath.

"No, ma'am."

"Elizabeth," I corrected.

"Uh, no. This Royal Burger isn't a franchise. The company—Royal Burger—owns it. We don't pay rent to anybody. And I've never even heard of Family Restaurants or Pacific Properties. On the expense end, we pay salaries and operating costs and return a percentage of profit to Royal Burger corporate each month. But—"

He stopped, thinking.

"But what?"

"Well, if this place was to pay rent, that's an awfully high number there, don't you think?"

The check had been drawn against one of California's larger banks, at a branch in nearby Poway. I figured I'd look into that on my way back to the city later. Right now I had one more call to make in rustic Ramona.

34

I had consulted my Thomas Brothers map again before heading out to Silver Branch Road. Now I reached into my purse for the other map, the cosmic one. Once again the cluster of planets in Scorpio popped out at me, Venus in particular. At first I'd thought this feminine planet might represent Janice's stepmother. Tanya, Alan's old girlfriend and the only other significant female I knew of in Janice's universe, had seemed a long shot. Geographically, she certainly was. But Janice's universe was getting smaller all the time. I started the engine and pulled out onto the dusty highway.

The miles seemed to stretch longer this trip, probably because I didn't have my CDs and the Charger's radio picked up nothing but a staticky country western station. I was beginning to wonder if I'd passed it altogether when at last I spotted the place. The lone house, wrecked on a shore of junk in a sea of desert sand, looked so forlorn it nearly broke my heart. I pulled the Charger into the empty, unpaved driveway.

I stood on the tiny cement block that served as a front porch and hollered through the screen door. "Hello! Is anybody home?"

Out of nowhere a large pair of eyes peered at me through the screen. She wore a dirty white knit top over a pair of pink pants that were too tight in the waist and too short at the ankle. Her bangs needed cutting and her shoulder-length hair could have used a brush. I pegged her at about seven, and growing fast.

"Hi there," I said.

"Mom and Jay aren't home," she said flatly.

Mom and Jay. The name Jay rang a bell here. Wasn't that the name of the guy Alan had introduced to Janice's boss when Ellis had wanted to buy drugs? Frizzy hair? Could Jay be the name of the gnome from the bachelor pad, my friend from the beach? Theoretically, of course, it was possible that the name Jay was a coincidence here. Then, too, the sun could, theoretically, fail to rise tomorrow.

"Jay is your mom's boyfriend, right?"

The little girl nodded.

"Will they be back soon?"

She shrugged her tiny shoulders. At that moment a gray cat walked up from behind me and began to rub my ankles. "Oh, I remember you," I said, reaching to stroke the cat. "Well, look at that. You've had your babies." I scratched under her chin and she extended her neck, begging for more. "Can I see your kitties?" I asked the little girl.

"Jay flushed 'em."

"What?"

"They came out of her behind, so he flushed them," she explained, not sounding quite so convinced herself.

"Where are your mom and her boyfriend?" I asked, trying to control my anger.

"I dunno."

"You don't know? Did they go to the store? Did they go to work?"

"I don't know." She sounded a little scared, as if she were giving the wrong answer but didn't know any other one.

I softened my voice. "Well, honey, do you know when they'll be home?"

"No." I could barely hear her.

"They didn't tell you?"

"No."

I let out an exasperated sigh. Leaving a child like this. I intended to follow up with Child Protective Services, but not this afternoon.

"Will you be okay, alone here?"

"Yeah."

"Is there a neighbor or someone you can go to, if you need help?"

She pouted her wet little lips and shrugged. "I guess so."

"Okay, my name is Elizabeth. What's yours?"

"Katie."

"Okay, Katie, I'm going to leave for a little while, but I'll be back later. Have you had any lunch?"

"I have Cocoa Krispies," she said. For the first time a smile broke through her gloom.

I wished I could take her with me, but that would jeopardize the investigation. Katie had made it this far. She'd be all right for one more afternoon. Or so I prayed. "Do you want me to bring you anything?" I said.

She considered that for several seconds. "Barbie?" she asked hopefully.

I laughed. "I'll see what I can do. See you later."

I had just reached the Charger when it occurred to me to ask Katie about Huerte. I turned to see her still standing in the doorway staring at me. I grabbed the picture from my briefcase and walked it over to her.

"Hey, Katie, have you ever seen this man before?"

Her little eyebrows came together in deep concentration. "No, I have not," she announced decidedly.

About ten miles east of Ramona lies Julian, a town nestled in the mountains that separate San Diego County from the hard-core parched desert of Anza Borrego. Julian is an enchanting little tourist trap done up in Western themes: horse-drawn buggies in the middle of town, wooden sidewalks, swinging saloon doors. Just beyond Julian are the state parks of the Cleveland National Forest, magical California treasures filled with ancient oaks and Ponderosa pines. I made it a point to get up here at least twice a year, to take in the splendor of unspoiled wilderness. As long as I was this close today, I figured I might as well use my time wisely. While I was waiting for Tanya to return, I could renew my spirit by picking up a late lunch in Julian and dining in communion with Nature.

My first stop was in the General Store, the closest thing to a department store the little town has. A funky place like this in the middle of nowhere couldn't possibly have them, but just the same I asked the gingham-clad woman behind the counter if she happened to carry Barbie dolls.

"Of course we do!" she said and brought out the familiar plastic celebrity with the improbable figure. "That's her," I said, shaking my head. Well, if it would make the kid happy. . . .

My next stop was into the pie shop for Julian's famous apple pie à la mode. From there I went to the corner grocery, buying portable edibles—crackers, cheese, a nectarine—to stash in my purse. Before heading out to the forest, I used the pay phone to put in a call to McGowan's machine. I told him where I was, what I was up to, and not to expect me home until after dark; as there was no telling where Alan's former girlfriend had gone off to or how long she might be gone. I called the station and left a similar message with the dispatcher.

By now it was late in the afternoon. As I ascended the winding road through the pine-covered mountains I felt the acute clarity of perception that graces me every now and again. I had the distinct sense of being exactly where I was supposed to be. All the doubt and confusion I'd endured earlier in the week were now replaced by absolute calm and acceptance. I smiled to myself. Lenny Lenton would be proud of me.

I'd gathered a number of facts and knew I could be spending this time frantically trying to assemble them into a coherent scheme. But more than that, I knew this was not the time. I needed the peace and strength now more than the facts. The facts would be there, ready to unscramble, when the time was right.

I drove into the Cleveland National Forest and spent the remainder of the daylight hours soaking in the wisdom of the pines. At forty-five hundred feet above sea level, the altitude here was considerably greater than in town, and the temperature dropped off mercifully. Sitting cross-legged on a bed of pine needles near an enormous old oak, I began to polish off my nectarine, then thought to retrieve Janice's journal from my briefcase. Something in there, I knew, was calling for my attention.

The journal fell open to a page whose corner had been turned down. I glanced at it and recognized the passage I'd read that first day, when I had opened the book at random, the one that began, "He's killing me. I love sex as well as the next guy, but these four a.m. marathons have got to stop. . . ." Now that I knew about Alan's old drug habit, Janice's observation had new meaning.

A name farther down the same page caught my eye. I recognized this passage, too:

> It seems Alan has a past: a daughter from a previous union. She's six now and he goes on and on about how adorable she is. . . . He worries out loud about her some nights, says she doesn't live in the best of circumstances. . . . From what Alan says I guess his daughter's mother hangs out with a dealer now and is more or less of a low life. Her name is Tanya.

This was the page that had fallen open to me at the beginning of the investigation, when I was thinking how books sometimes open to the very passage one needs to read.

The first reference, about Alan, had initially put me onto *him* as the prime suspect. But here was Tanya's name, on the same page.

In that moment, staring down at the journal, I began to feel exposed. The wind sweeping through the tops of the pines overhead was the only sound, but now there was another presence here as well. Very near. Right over my shoulder. I could feel it as surely as if—

Janice? I thought silently. I turned around.

A blue jay, cawing loudly, swooped down from a pine bough to nab a treasure from an unsuspecting squirrel sitting on his hind legs at the base of the old oak. There was a brief tussle, a crashing of dried leaves, and the blue jay rose victoriously. The colorful birds, protected here, were beautiful but notorious pests.

The disturbance had broken the enchantment of the forest, and I knew it was time to go. I packed my things and headed back. As I drove down the mountain I was surprised to see that the landscape had already fallen into dusk. Storm clouds had gathered in the east. To the west the setting sun was rolling out a horizon of red through the summer smog, bloody gauze along the surface of a wounded earth.

35

By the time I reached Tanya's house it was pitch dark. We would have a nearly full moon in Scorpio sometime tonight, but it hadn't come up over the horizon yet. The Charger's high beams caught Tanya's mailbox and I slowed to turn in. I saw two small green disks flash in the blackness as the headlights illuminated the pupils of the gray cat. She was standing in the driveway, so I continued on past. A detached garage covered with aluminum siding stood just beyond the house. I parked on the far side of the garage, where the Charger was hidden from view. It was an afterthought, but a prudent one.

I slung my purse over my shoulder, got out of the car, and picked my way along the path through the junk in the front yard. The house was dark now. Someone had closed up the front door over the screen. I knocked twice with no response.

"Katie! Katie are you home?"

I waited a few seconds and knocked again. "Katie!"

I stepped down from the cement porch and tried to get a peek through the front window, but the house was shrouded in blackness. I couldn't make out even the vaguest of shapes inside, just black on black. Maybe somebody had come by and picked the kid up, taken her out to dinner. Or to the movies.

Yeah, right.

The humid night air hung too thick, too quiet in this place. The darkness was more than a matter of insufficient light. Darkness lingered here as a presence. For an instant I experienced the old, familiar horror I'd felt at the Bad House of my childhood.

Something brushed me and I let out a gasp. The cat, rubbing my ankle. "Good, God. You scared me, sweetheart," I whispered as I reached down to pet her. "Where's Katie, huh? Where'd your little friend go?" The cat meowed. It was a worried sound. Or maybe I was just projecting.

I tried knocking again, then gave the doorknob a twist. It opened without a sound. "Katie?" I called through the screen. The smell of stale pot smoke escaped through the open door. As my eyes adjusted to the blackness, I was able to make out the entryway and the shadowy living room beyond.

"Katie?"

I knew she was here, somewhere. I *knew*. That alarmed me. Another left brain/right brain argument began. My logical side argued, quite cogently I thought, that this wasn't the safest place to be spending a Friday night, and besides, to proceed would constitute breaking and entering. This is police work, it's not in my job description, et cetera. The other part of me said, *There's no time for that now, she needs you, you can do this*. I was really just standing there listening to the relative merits of each pleading when something quite beyond a decision propelled me through the door. My feet simply moved.

I stepped inside and searched with my hand for a light along the right wall. Nothing. I slid my palm up and down along the wall to my left. Nothing. Tentatively, I stepped across the entryway, my hands outstretched, my fingertips groping. Shuffling through the dark like this reminded me how much I'd hated being blindfolded as a kid and forced to pin the tail on the donkey at all those silly birthday parties.

One step, two steps, three steps, four steps . . .

My shin knocked into something hard on the eighth step. Reaching down, I felt a table. My fingers found a lamp and switched it on.

In the dim glow of a forty-watt bulb, the living room reappeared just as I'd remembered it: impossibly cluttered. The bhang still sat among magazines, dishes, and dirty ashtrays on the coffee table. There didn't appear to be a soul around.

Under the lamp, a check stub caught my eye. It had been issued from the County of San Diego Social Services Department, aka welfare. The recipient's name was Jason Drum. Jay. *Jay is your mom's boyfriend, is that right?* Any relation to Rob Rhymes-with-Scum Drum? How many Drums in San Diego County? Coincidence?

No coincidences.

I turned to the left. The light ended where the darkened hallway began.

"Katie?"

I braved the black hallway. Once again I made my way slowly, groping for a light switch. As I walked I slid my hand along the right wall. Without warning, my fingers slipped into a void, an open doorway. Along the inside wall of the room I found a light switch at last. As I flipped it on, bright light from an overhead fixture exposed the room in harsh detail. It was small and windowless. Furnished with only a twin bed. Several cardboard boxes were lying about. An open suitcase sat on the bed. There was no closet. No Katie.

The suitcase was either half packed or half unpacked. A woman's clothes—halter tops, bikini underpants—were strewn across the bed, together with little-girl things—miniature pants, miniature T-shirts, tiny thong sandals.

I turned out the light and ventured back into the darkened hall. The way was narrow. This time I stretched my arms wide, skimming the walls on each side of me. My left hand found an opening. Inside my fingers found another light switch. This time a light above the sink revealed a small, dirty bathroom. Mildewed vinyl shower curtain, empty bathtub.

"Katie?" I called out to comfort myself with the sound of a human voice as much as anything else. Tanya had been packing a suitcase. Going where? Why? Maybe she needed something for her trip and had taken Katie to the store with her. Maybe I was just trespassing here. Maybe this urgency I felt for the child was imaginary.

Yeah, right.

I switched off the light, backed out of the bathroom, and continued down the hallway. Toward the end I found another doorway on the right. There was a sliding lock on the outside of the door, too high for a child to reach. I slid the bolt open, figuring this for a master bedroom where adults did things they did not wish children to see.

The smell was the first thing to hit me. Not ammonia, but equally unpleasant and pungent. A metallic, acidic smell, like synthetic citrus gone bad. The room was dimly lit by some grow lights in the corner, where a few pot plants were coming along nicely. Perhaps a dozen twenty-gallon glass containers lined an entire wall. They looked like the bottles the Culligan man brings each week, but this was no stash of mountain fresh water. Rubber tubes affixed to the tops of the bottles were siphoning a chemical substance the color of anemic blood into the huge glass containers. In the middle of the room there was a folding metal chair draped with a T-shirt. It was a black T-shirt, the wings of the Harley-Davidson emblem emblazoned across the chest.

No coincidences.

Cold was running along my spine like mercury up a thermometer. I very much wanted to be anywhere but here. Already, though, I could hear voices rising in the hallway.

36

I was eight years old again. "It" was counting to ten. I had to hide, and hide fast. Once upon a time this meth lab had been a bedroom. The clothes closet was just steps away. I dashed into it, nestled in the dark corner, and shut the door just as Jay and Tanya entered the lab. About that time I became an adult again and remembered the gun in my purse.

". . . not going anywhere, fucking bitch."

I recognized Jay's voice. It was meaner and more threatening than usual tonight. I couldn't make out Tanya's answer, but I thought I heard whimpering. Hard to tell, as her quieter voice was muffled through the closed closet door. Jay's voice, amplified in anger, came over loud and clear.

"Think you can fucking bullshit me, huh?"

I thought I heard Tanya say something about wanting to "get away with Katie for a little while." It didn't seem to be what Jay wanted to hear.

"Fuck you, you lying bitch."

"Just a little while, Jay! . . . don't care . . . can have everything! . . . to see my mama, Jay . . ."

Their voices lowered and for several minutes I couldn't make out the conversation. By now I'd found the Glock in my purse and held it ready. My body was shaking but my mind was at ease. I'd love to credit my masterful, Zenlike consciousness for this relative serenity, but I think it had more to do with the semiautomatic weapon in my hand.

Like the rest of my generation I've seen entirely too much television, so I couldn't suppress a ridiculous image of myself bursting from this closet, holding the drug dealers at gunpoint, and saving the day. In reality I'd just as soon have jumped in front of a speeding train. My mom has always told me: When you don't know what to do next, it's best to do nothing. So that's basically what I did for the next ten minutes or so.

A lot of thoughts crossed my mind as I crouched in that closet, fighting off a leg cramp. I thought about how excellent this scam was, as scams go. Jay and Janice's old boss had a nearly perfect setup. The property was paid up, no bank or outside owner to meddle in affairs. Jay could make his crystal meth with relative assurance of privacy. His partner, Stan Ellis, had until now succeeded in laundering the profits through a legitimate real estate conglomerate. What a team. I contemplated their revenues. McGowan had said that a pound of crystal has a street value around $20,000 these days, that a good lab produced about four hundred pounds a month. Could this lab manufacture that much? Easily, was my guess. After a little multiplication I came up with about $8 million for a good month, close to $100 mill a year. Divide by two for Murphy's Law, and still . . .

Would people kill for that amount? Far less, usually.

Huerte's bungalow in Pacific Beach must have been the lab's marketing arm on the coast. That would explain Huerte always paying his rent on time, in cash. Huerte had found some choice roommates in Rob and Jay Drum, that was sure.

I wondered how Janice had caught on to Stan's involvement. She'd obviously discovered something amiss in the account books at Pacific Properties. Then she discovered the skeleton property in Ramona, the one owned by her father's corporation, not by Pacific Properties. She would have wondered where the "rent" money was really coming from. But how had she unearthed the real source of revenue, this lovely hellhole here at 1037 Silver Branch Road? Perhaps Alan had told Janice, as he had told me, that Stan not only was a drug user but also was actively seeking a connection. Maybe Stan had tipped his own hand by revealing his acquaintance with Jay to Janice, or by casually offering Janice some recreational drugs.

Janice had gathered enough evidence to make an appointment with a vice cop. Had Janice been to this place? I had the distinct feeling I was retracing her steps exactly.

A fracas outside the closet door interrupted my thoughts. There was no mistaking the sound of human flesh hitting human flesh. I heard a thud on the carpet and then sobbing.

"Fucking lying bitch."

"You're scaring me, Jay!" Tanya's voice rose in fear. Her every word was high pitched and clear. "You're losing it!" she screamed. "You can't just *off* people who get in your way! You're getting totally paranoid! You are really blowing it, big time!"

"The blonde had our number, Tanya." Jay had the deadly sound of a man who'd already run out of patience. "She was here, man. She knew. She was going to the cops. Everything I have here was at stake. Everything *you* have, you stupid bitch. You fucking stupid bitch!"

More sickening thuds.

"But you didn't have to kill Michael!" Tanya was sobbing uncontrollably now, gulping for breath.

"Does it hurt, baby? Does it hurt that the guy who fucked you is dead?" Jay was sneering cruelly, relishing the torture.

"I didn't fuck him!"

"Lying fucking cunt!"

I thought I heard a boot hitting flesh and the sound of Tanya retching. Now I had a genuine urge to burst from the closet and stop the violence, but one misplaced bullet could turn this meth lab into toxic waste and us along with it. I forced myself to keep a cool head, to detach from Tanya's dilemma and pull some facts together. How had Pia described Michael Huerte? A handsome ladies' man? Whether he'd bedded Tanya or not, flirting with her in front of Jay apparently had been his fatal mistake. Setting up the car accident, Jay and Stan had gotten rid of two troublesome interlopers in one fell swoop.

The full weight of a human body thudded against the wall. Tanya cried out for mercy. There was no fight left in her voice, just terror. "St-stop! You're too high, Jay! Stop! You're losing it! It's the drugs, baby! You're *too high!*"

"You're the one with the fucking *problem*, man! You-fucking-nympho-maniac!" I could hear deliberate, rhythmic thumping as Jay punctuated his words with kicks to her flesh. It was happening just a few feet away from me, near the wall to the left. My stomach lurched.

Then there was a sound of clinking glass, and my heart froze. I pushed away a terribly real vision of this lab exploding. I could feel the sweat beading on my upper lip. My heart was booming.

A gagging reflex kicked in and I swallowed my own bile. I don't know if it was the fear, or the stench of the place. Even from inside the closet, the atmosphere was getting to me. This, I thought, is what hell smells like. Not rotting bodies, but the stench of toxic chemicals, the manufacturing of heartaches.

"I'm done with you, man," I heard Jay say. Then the room was quiet.

37

My clothes, far closer to wet than dry, felt as if they were glued to my skin. I was so hot I was sure I had a fever. For the past several minutes I'd been fighting off an urge to vomit, and now breathing was becoming difficult. But what finally ejected me from the damn closet was a horrifying attack of claustrophobia. I took a deep breath and came out with my gun drawn.

The room was empty.

Now I had a quandary on my hands. I couldn't very well stroll back out through the front door. Chances were good Tanya and Jay had advanced their warfare into the living room. But as far as I knew that front door was the only exit from this deathtrap. I was standing there trying to figure my next step when I heard a dreadfully familiar sound—the report of a rifle.

The shot had been fired from behind the house.

Then I heard another boom, followed by a broad, low rumbling. Thunder. The glass bottles along the wall vibrated slightly.

I knew with certainty that trying to get out the way I'd come in would end in disaster. The hallway outside the bedroom door loomed as menacingly as a thousand-foot fall, a blazing fire, or any other certain death. Jay must be coming back into the house. He must be the death I sensed coming down the hallway.

I dashed across the meth lab to a large window on the north wall. It would have to do. The glass slid open without a struggle. I was grateful that there was no screen. I looped my purse strap securely over my shoulder, then boosted myself up, draped my leg over, and rolled through. I landed in a pile of smelly papers and cartons.

The blackness of the night was now my ally. I darted in and out among boxes, crates, car parts. Visibility was low, but as far as I could tell the shadowy shapes of junk spread out over at least an acre back here. I moved quickly and encountered just one problem—an impregnable wooden fence, probably ten feet high, surrounding the yard.

For a moment I panicked, but then calmed myself with the fact that the gnome Jay didn't seem to be in hot pursuit. Come to think of it, he had no reason even to suspect I was back here. Crouching behind a disemboweled old sofa, I started thinking about how I might assemble some of the junk lying around into a ladder of sorts. I was just getting optimistic enough to move the sofa when Jay's frizzy silhouette appeared against the lighted lab window.

I'd left the lab window open!

Extending from Jay's darkened form was the long barrel of a rifle, probing the yard like a hungry mechanical serpent. As he turned, I could also make out a scope on top of the barrel. A laser scope, no doubt.

I had the Glock, true. But a Glock is a handgun, not intended for long-distance target shooting. I'm not a bad shot, but I'd never really even practiced with McGowan's gun. If I were to take a shot in the dark at Jay, the fire from my barrel would immediately reveal my position. If I missed, his job would be easy. In short, I was outarmed.

Jay was now striding confidently through the debris toward the back of the yard. Heading in my direction.

As quietly as possible I crept around the sofa and began to make my way farther back. I had taken cover behind some garbage cans and hollowed-out car shells and was beginning to pick up momentum when the worst possible thing happened: I tripped and fell. Pitching forward, I knew there was no way I could land noiselessly. My heart began to pound its deafening beat, and I found myself prone, facedown in stinking garbage, utterly unable to move.

I don't know how long I'd been lying there, frozen. Already this nightmare had stretched beyond the point of bearability. I was aware only that my hearing had returned, sharper than ever. I picked up the sound of a footstep, much closer now. I sent a silent prayer: *Over to you, God.*

A loud clattering, like an aluminum can falling on metal, echoed from somewhere across the yard. I heard scuffling nearby, the report of the rifle, the unmistakable yowling of a cat. Something—pieces of something—hit the ground perhaps fifty feet away. Jay's footsteps hurried toward the noise. I pulled myself to my knees, took a deep breath, and crawled in the opposite direction. The shell of an old pickup truck loomed just a few feet ahead. I scrambled toward it and dove for cover hands first.

My palms skidded to a stop on something soft and slick and rubbery warm. I fought back an urge to scream. Tanya's body lay faceup, her chest one massive exit wound. I reminded myself I was not squeamish about human anatomy. *You're not squeamish, Elizabeth. We'll wash our hands later.*

This was obviously not an intelligent place to hang out. I set my sights on what looked like the front end of a Volkswagen bus and ran low and fast. I sneaked into the dark hollow of its wrecked dashboard and had the scare of my life.

Another body, this one alive. Katie looked up at me with eyes as round as full moons. She was terrified, but not paralyzed by shock. I looked at her intently, pressing my index finger against my lips hard. She nodded as if to say, "I know, I know." I huddled down with her and she pressed her little shoulders tightly against mine.

The footsteps were returning now.

As if a switch had been thrown, the entire desert sky lit

up with a silver flash of lightning. The shapes of junk in the yard were illuminated for a brief moment, a single frame from a black-and-white horror movie. A thunderclap exploded in our ears. The air was thick with pent-up moisture. I don't know how hot it was, exactly. I only know I have never sweated so much, before or since.

Maybe it was the lightning that set Jay off. He began shooting into the yard, firing at a steady pace but aiming at random. A bullet occasionally zinged against the metal car parts or thwacked into an old piece of furniture, sometimes close by, sometimes not. Mostly we heard just the crack from the rifle, again and again and again. After an eternity of stress, the firing stopped. I then thought I heard a small sound carrying across the yard—empty clicking. It was followed by the high-pitched, nasal cursing of a poor sport.

"God*damn* it."

For a moment all was quiet. I heard Jay mumble something like "shit." Then, in a raised voice, "Pia, bring me those two-twenty shells."

Had I heard that right?

"Pia! Bring me the reloads!" Insistent now and clear as a bell.

He waited for a moment, then whined again. "God*damn* it!"

I heard his footsteps walking away. I peeked around the front end of the Volkswagen and watched him disappear into the house.

"Stay here," I whispered to Katie. "I'll be back for you." As an afterthought, I pulled the Barbie from my purse and handed it to her. She clung to it.

I moved as close to the house as I dared. When I got within twenty-five feet I settled in behind another car shell. I had a clear view of the lab inside. Through the open window I could see the glass bottles of methamphetamine lining the wall. Then I saw Jay enter the room. And behind him, Pia.

Tonight Pia was dressed in jeans and a tank top. Her long brown hair had been pulled up under a baseball cap, but there was no mistaking her flawless posture, her ballerina's carriage.

I stared at her, disbelieving, the way I remember staring at my unringing telephone when I was in the ninth grade and my first boyfriend stood me up for a dance. How could I have misread Pia so completely? Too late I saw how her beauty had disarmed me. She'd seen it, though, and had totally put me together. Literally. I was still wearing the lapis earrings she'd given me. Perhaps they'd fallen from the crown of Lucifer after all.

I racked the Glock. *Well, Pia, we're really dancing now.*

Jay walked to the far wall and opened the closet. Ironic, I thought, that I'd earlier been hiding in the very spot he kept his ammunition. Pia reached to the top shelf, helping him search for the bullets.

For a moment none of what was happening seemed real to me. In a daze I stared as Pia pulled down a box, opened it, passed the bullets to Jay. It all looked like a silent movie: their animated conversation, Jay's agitated reloading of the rifle. Their actions seemed to have nothing to do with me, the curious onlooker.

A sudden knowledge pierced my reverie: *Jay is about to die.* Eerily, he seemed to hear my thoughts. He turned from Pia and peered into the night, directly at me. He took a step forward, raised the rifle to his shoulder, and pointed through the open window. I made direct eye contact with the eye of the barrel.

I had no time to aim. I simply pointed and fired, three deafening rounds. The bullets hit the bottles of methamphetamine lining the wall behind Jay. I saw two of the glass containers shatter, then watched in horror as the others disintegrated in a domino effect.

Jay and Pia instantly dropped out of view, too fast to see.

One moment they had been standing, in the next second they were gone. I prayed that the walls of the house would contain the deadly toxins of the lab long enough for Katie and me to escape.

On wobbly legs and shaking knees, I made my way back to the little girl. Katie was waiting right where I'd left her. I squeezed her shoulder and then with violently trembling hands, started to pull the old sofa against the fence.

"Why are you doing that?" she asked.

"We need to get out of here as fast as we can," I said. My voice was shaking, too.

"There's a gate right over here," she stated. She took me by the hand and pulled me through the yard.

The sky opened just as we reached the gate. All night the atmosphere had been deadly still. I felt one fat warning drop hit my forearm, then suddenly there was so much water singing through the air I could hardly hear. I had no desire to shelter myself from the cloudburst. I desperately needed the cooling. I needed the cleansing, too. I felt I could stand in the rain all night and never wash clean.

We ran through the downpour to the opposite side of the garage. I found the keys to the Charger in my pocket and opened the door for Katie. She scrambled into the front seat and I leaned my back against the side of the car. I felt the water pummeling my head, soaking my scalp. For a minute my vision got spotty and I was certain I would black out. I took a deep breath of rain-soaked air and closed my eyes. When I opened them I saw whirling patterns of red and blue. Still I couldn't move. I simply leaned against the car, powerless, drenched now.

Through the sheets of rain I watched a glowing patch of light begin to take form. Hovering bright and yellow, it began to move toward me. Coming nearer, a man in a yellow plastic parka. The next thing I knew I was surrounded by a pair of enormous arms.

"Tom, how did you—"

"When I heard your phone message, I knew," he said, pulling me close and cupping my head up under his chin. "I just *knew*."

EPILOGUE

⟨C⟩

The San Diego County coroner estimated that Jay and Pia died of toxic asphixiation within three minutes of the explosion. I told McGowan the whole story; he helped me with the edited version I gave in my statements to the police. ("Think of it as saving taxpayers' money," he said.) He assured me I had acted in self-defense, well within the course and scope of my professional duties. And that has been the official consensus, as well.

A special enforcement unit—officers so protectively garbed they looked more like astronauts than cops—had to be sent in from San Diego to contend with the mess. One of them found the body of the gray kitty near the house with most of a hind leg blown off. I wept at the news, at the same time experiencing the sober gratitude a soldier must feel when a buddy has saved his life and in so doing lost his own. The Ramona property was condemned and at the time of this writing, two weeks later, remains off bounds to what little drive-by traffic heads out that way.

The cleanup operation has extended to the human mess as well. Jay's brother, Rob Drum, was collared when he came in to identify Jay's body the day after the explosion. The idiot was carrying a quarter gram in his wallet. Stan Ellis has not yet been placed under arrest, but an intensive police investigation is closing in on him. I understand he's quite irritated by the team of federal auditors that has set up camp in the accounting department at Pacific Properties. His aura, I imagine, is burning bright red about now.

Those of us who were wounded by the ordeal have begun the slow road to healing. To my great relief Katie went into Alan's custody after a brief intervention by Child Protective Services. She may have gained a loving father, but Katie lost a mother, however unfit. To a child, destiny may deal no greater blow than the death of a parent. Having witnessed Tanya's violent demise, Katie begins her young life with a terrible disadvantage. I pray she'll be one of those who grow stronger through adversity.

My own torment comes and goes. A canine search of Pia Mia's beach boutique turned up a healthy inventory of crystal, neatly packed and ready for market in self-sealing glassine baggies. The fact that Pia was actively involved in the drug ring does not diminish my anguish about her death. Logically, I understand that I pulled that trigger to save not just my life, but Katie's as well. The realization refuses to console me. Like so many drug victims, Pia was in the wrong place, at the wrong time, with the wrong friends.

I went out to the beach at dawn the day after the meth lab exploded. The storm was clearing, and several broken-up thunderheads scudded across the ocean panorama. At this hour the shore was nearly deserted and the water was cool. I swam out far beyond the breakers, where the water was deep, and spent God knows how long floating on my back, watching the occasional pelican wing by, gazing through the gray and white clouds into the infinite blue above.

When my limbs grew tired I reached up to my earlobes and removed the lapis earrings. One by one I dropped them into the water, where they sank into the mystery. I reached back and unhooked the top of my cobalt-blue bathing suit, then squiggled out of the bottoms and released them onto the ocean surface. The garments floated for a few moments, then were drawn under by the subtle action of the waves. I watched their undulating descent into the underwater world. When the vivid blue pieces were completely enveloped by the steely sea, I swam slowly back to shore, allowing the waves to do most of the work.

As planned, McGowan met me at the shoreline with a large towel. He blocked the view from the beach while I wrapped the terry cloth around my body, then hugged me and had the good sense to say nothing. We stood in the surf for several minutes, the waves rushing around our calves. Finally he turned to me.

"I just want to know one thing."

I stared up at him, at the luminous energy surrounding him.

"Okay. One thing."

"You *really* can't tell me what color my aura is?"

I had to smile. "I think it's white, but I must warn you—"

"Yes?"

"Love is surely color-blind."

In all of New York's Chinatown, there is no one like P.I. Lydia Chin, who has a nose for trouble, a disapproving Chinese mother, and a partner named Bill Smith who's been living above a bar for sixteen years.

Hired to find some precious stolen porcelain, Lydia follows a trail of clues from highbrow art dealers into a world of Chinese gangs. Suddenly, this case has become as complex as her community itself—and as deadly as a killer on the loose...

China Trade

S. J. Rozan